A Christmas City Christmas
By
Larry L. Deibert

CAROLINA,
ENJOY

ISBN 9781795509961

Front cover photograph by Desha Utsick

Rear cover photograph by Cynthia Davies

Acknowledgements

I would like to thank the following people for contributing their stories to this book.

Karen Samuels
Randy Mixter
Robert Green
Christine Held
Tom Remely
Rich Ehrhart
Jeff Wartluft
Michael Larkin
Mark Casey

I would like to thank the following who have appeared as themselves in this book.

Rev. Dr. Marnie Mullen Crumpler,   Grace Church, Bethlehem, Pa.
Rev. Dr. Mark Crumpler, Grace Church, Bethlehem, Pa.
Billy Kounoupis, Billy's Downtown Diner
Sherrl Wilhide, Waitress at Brass Rail, Allentown, Pa.
Jessica Weida, Manager, Moravian Book Shop, Bethlehem, Pa.
Rick Bachl, St. Nicholas at Christmasfest Market, Bethlehem, Pa.
Mark Talijan, St. Nicholas at Christmasfest Market, Bethlehem, Pa.
Nicole Mertz, Journalist, The Morning Call, Allentown, Pa.
Bruce Haines, Managing Partner, Historic Hotel Bethlehem, Bethlehem, Pa.
Daniel Roebuck, Actor, Producer, Director, Bethlehem, Pa.
Deborah Helms, Bethlehem, Pa.

I would like to thank the following for their input to this story

Mark DiLuzio, Chief of Police, Bethlehem, Pa.
Dennis Costello, Manager, Historic Hotel Bethlehem, Bethlehem, Pa.
Kayla Dwyer, Journalist, The Morning Call, Bethlehem, Pa.

I would like to thank my editors, Edward Gibney, Linda Berghold, George Roman and Peggy Deibert for their input and corrections.

I would like to thank my Beta readers, Heather Newman, George Roman

Thanks to Jennifer Bradley, award winning author for creating another great cover.

December 20th, 2018

1

Retired Bethlehem Police Detective, Hyram Lasky, unlocked his store and strolled inside. Since opening in the spring, *Lasky's Health* had attracted a large customer base in the city, along with a significant number of online shoppers. He had become acutely aware of his physical well-being after losing his legs in an explosion at the restaurant where his retirement was being celebrated, nearly two years ago.

Lasky learned everything he could about fitness and health, especially the use of vitamins, supplements, food, and drink, along with exercises everyone could do to become more physically strong and healthy.

He sold all types of health products and held classes at several fitness centers because he had limited space in his small store.

Hyram turned off the alarm and switched on the lights. Seeing his wife hurrying down the street, he opened the door for her.

Susan Mitchell-Lasky gave him a smile as she scurried into the warm store. "Wow, its cold as hell out there, Hy." She gave him a peck on the cheek as she passed by.

"Yeah, it is. I thought you were coming over later," he said as he closed the door to the cold.

She hung her coat in the small closet. Her black prosthetic right arm hung limply at her side. Susan was a reporter for the Saucon Valley Press at the time of the explosion. She was Hyram's date at the restaurant the day of the explosion and she lost her arm in the blast. It took her only a short amount of time to become comfortable with a man-made arm, incredibly fortunate to be alive, and to have the opportunity to spend the rest of her life with her husband.

He was behind the counter setting up the cash drawer when she came up behind him. She threw her arms around him and said, "You know I love you more every day, Hyram Lasky."

Lasky nodded, smiled, and turned around to wrap his arms around her. "Love you more, Susan."

They kissed just as Harold Gibbons, their lone employee, hurried into the store. "Jeez, guys, get a room, will ya."

"Mornin', Hal," they offered in unison. Susan said, "How are your wedding plans coming along?"

Hal hung his coat in the small closet, turned to them and said, "Excellent. Jim and I booked a ballroom at the *Hotel Bethlehem*, although we can't get in until February. We're talking to florists, bands, and photographers, and I'm sure we will have everything ready to go long before the ceremony."

"That's great, Hal. You guys have been together forever, and it's wonderful that you can finally tie the knot."

As Hal stocked the shelves, he replied, "It sure is. We could have married two years ago, but we both wanted to offer an amazing event for our friends and family. The coolest thing is that we've been together for almost ten years, and we've been accepted in the community for most of that time. Occasionally his buddies at the fire department would harass him, but he knew it was mainly in good fun." Jim Weissman had been a firefighter for seven years.

The doorbell chimed the arrival of customers. Three women, longtime Bethlehem residents stepped through the door. Hyram greeted them with a hearty 'Merry Christmas and Happy Hanukkah'. Two of the women were

Christian and the other was a devout Jew. The staff of *Lasky's Health* always tried to offer the appropriate greeting.

"Merry Christmas to you all," one of the ladies chimed out through a huge smile.

Suddenly, a Hanukkah song began to play through the store's speakers. Susan directed Alexa to play the song for their Jewish customer and friend, Miriam Ickowicz. She was an attorney in the firm of Ickowicz, Lieberman and Zucker. They specialized in divorce and injury cases and were respected throughout the Lehigh Valley. She nodded and mouthed "Thank you," and then went about her shopping.

After the handful of Hanukkah songs played, Hyram directed Alexa to play Christmas songs. As he listened to *Holly Jolly Christmas* for the umpteenth thousand time in his life, Hy wished he had a nickel for every time he heard the booming voice of *Burl Ives*, among others.

There were fifteen customers in the shop now, so Hy and Susan were both behind the counter, preparing to check them out. As they waited, the doorbell chimed, and Jack Mann, their happy-go-lucky mailman, entered the store with his usual greeting of, 'Hi, Hy, hi, Susan.' He smiled every time he said that, making Hy always wonder if he was a brick or two short of a full wheelbarrow.

Of course, the store owners got payback when they said, "Hi, Jack."

Jack paged through the mail as he slowly made his way to the counter. He took a moment to read a postcard, because reading postcards was something that many of his fellow carriers enjoyed doing. He stopped in front of the counter, handing Susan the stack of bills, Christmas cards, assorted pamphlets, and magazines. "You guys got a nice card from the Wrights. They have had a couple of nice trips since shutting down the inn, and they're preparing for a nice Christmas holiday with their family." Steve and Mary Wright owned the Carolina Temple Island Inn, in Wrightsville Beach, North Carolina, where Hy and Susan had hoped to spend a nice, quiet vacation last year. They wound up taking on three witches, hundreds of ghosts, and a bunch of werewolves on the deck of the battleship North Carolina instead.

"So, Jack, do you always read your patrons' mail or just ours?" Susan inquired, teasingly.

"Oh, I like to read every postcard I can. If a carrier gets a really interesting one, he or she will usually share it with the other carriers on each side of his case at work." A mailman's case was a three-sided metal structure, consisting of five or six vertical rows of individual or double slots where the outgoing mail was cased in delivery order and then pulled down for delivery.

Jack grabbed a cookie from the plate on the counter as Hy asked, "How's Brian Miller doing? I haven't seen him since we met at a Lehigh football game in October."

"He's doing fine as far as I know, bitching about the job every day. I don't know why he is still working, though. He is worth beaucoup bucks. You may not have seen him because he and Jessie bought a historic Bethlehem home. I looked it up, and it cost them almost a mil."

"I didn't know that. I guess I should give them a call soon and get together for a beer. I toured some of those homes a couple a years ago. They are really cool." Hy replied.

Jack finished his cookie as four customers came to the counter. "Okay, see you guys. I gotta run."

When Jack left, Hy let out a sigh. He was thinking about Christmas Day eight years ago. Before the vampire had been slain, he grappled with the fact that vampires did exist. Although there was hard evidence about *only* one, he was relieved when the paranormal threat ended.

2

On that Christmas morning, he had been enjoying a cup of coffee when the phone rang.

"Merry Christmas. Lasky residence."

As he listened to the caller carefully, his hands began to shake. Fumbling the receiver back into its cradle, he hurried to the bedroom, got dressed, and was out the door in less than five minutes.

Twenty-five minutes later he parked his car at the side of the road where a policeman stood awaiting his arrival. The cop walked him down a path through a thickly wooded area to a field where several police officers and Everett Gardner, the coroner, were staring at what appeared, from the distance, to be many body parts. Hyram also saw a great deal of blood splashed over the snowy landscape.

He finally was close enough to see that there were three bodies-two men and a woman-ripped to shreds. Lasky felt bile rise in his throat, and he quickly turned away as vomit spewed from his mouth. When he recovered, he turned back to the bodies then looked at Gardner. "What the hell happened here, Ev?"

"I'm the one who discovered the bodies. After a quick examination, I called for some officers to help me transport them back to the coroner's office. Then I called you."

Lasky saw that the officers were pale, with evidence on their faces and their jackets that they had lost their breakfasts, as well. He looked at Gardner again, his face ashen. "Vampires?"

Gardner slowly shook his head.

Hyram relaxed just a bit. "What then, Ev? Who could have done something like this?"

"Well, that's the thing, Hy. This wasn't done by any person or people. Look around and tell me what you see."

The detective looked the bodies over closely and saw definite bite marks. Body parts had been ripped from the bodies by something that possessed tremendous strength. Then he saw what Everett had wanted him to see; and he spewed again, looking back at Everett, shaking his head. He was staring at the footprints in the snow.

"Yes, Hy. Those tracks are exactly what you think they are, even though there are none in Pennsylvania. And look at the size of them. I honestly believe these three people were attacked by one or more wolves – large wolves."

"Are you certain?"

"As certain as I can be at this stage; but after what we have all been through, I'm going to venture a guess that we are dealing with wolves with super strength, wolves that walk on their hind legs..."

"You're not going to tell me...?"

"Walk with me."

They followed the wolf tracks a few hundred yards away from the bodies, where the imprints suddenly disappeared, replaced by the tracks of two barefooted humans.

Hiram Lasky dropped to his knees.

The vampire was dead. Now he and his men would have to find and kill two werewolves.

3

Susan watched her husband, knowing that he was recalling when the werewolves were in Bethlehem three years ago. It seemed like yesterday sometimes, and the memories stayed sharp.

She had been taking a break in her car near the cornfield where a body had been found. One police officer and a man in a suit, probably a detective she thought, were looking at a lump in the cornfield. Susan, a reporter for *The Saucon Press* assumed that the lump was a body, but she was too far away to conclude that for sure until the coroner pulled up with his hearse.

They loaded the remains in the back of the vehicle; and when the cops and the coroner left the scene, she took a walk to see if she could find anything unusual, or just something that they missed.

Susan kicked up a phone, covered by some dead corn stalks, and when she turned it on, she was shocked out of her mind. She saw a picture of a large, blonde wolf charging the person who last held the phone.

Later that day she went to Hyram's office and confronted him with her evidence, giving her a one-up over all the newshounds that would soon find out about werewolves in the Christmas city.

After the wolves were destroyed, Hyram retired. That night a party for him was being held and when everyone was inside, enjoying the food and drink, three people stood outside with detonators. Three bombs went off inside, killing six and wounding seventeen. That was how she lost her right arm.

Over the next six months, Susan fell in love with Hyram, and a nearly thirty-year age difference meant nothing.

She would love him until the day she died.

4

On the south side of Bethlehem, Brian Miller stopped delivering mail so he could answer a phone call. "Hi, Jess, what's up?"

"Not much. I'm heading out to do some serious Christmas shopping, and I wondered if you'd like to come to Christmasfest Market after work to join me."

"I wish I could, but I have to look up a carrier and help him out. I won't be finished till about seven. Plus, rain is coming in, and if it's raining hard, it will take me even longer."

"You know, you don't have to put in all those hours anymore.

"I know, but I still love the job enough to put up with all the extraneous BS they throw at me. My bitching in the office is just a stress reliever. Once I'm out on the street, it's all good."

"Alright, I'll see you later. Have a great day."

"You too."

He continued his route; but during this season, his mind always took him back to 2010 when he and Jess were in the thick of the vampire hunt. After they found out who the vampire was, they figured the hunting would be easier; but it actually became more difficult. He still had shakes eight years later, but he never told his wife. They rarely talked about that time anymore, and he wondered if it was time to get some therapy.

Brian could retire in eight more years with a great pension, along with health insurance-a must in today's world. By then, he would have thirty years of service and he would only be sixty years old.

After the vampire was slain, both he and Jessie were given a large sum of money to tell their story to several major magazines. They had also heard there was a movie in the making, but that fell through. At this time the couple was worth nine million dollars, and that is why they had bought the historic home on Market Street.

They had moved into the house at the beginning of last month. The home was nearly pristine, and they had very little work to do, apart from decorating it to their own tastes. It consisted of three floors and had a very large living room with a fireplace, dining room, kitchen, powder room, and a study on the first floor, three bedrooms and two baths on the second floor, and the third floor was converted into a spare room including a small bathroom.

The exterior included a two-sided sitting porch which was a great place to hang out.

His phone rang again. It was his supervisor. "What's up, Carl?"

"Good news for you, Brian. Eric decided he wanted to do his overtime, so you can eight and skate." An eight-hour workday would be very appreciative he thought.

"Thanks, Boss. Jess will be glad to hear that." He hung up, smiling from ear to ear. Carl Wakerley was one of the best supervisors he ever worked for, and he hoped he'd stay that way for the remainder of his career.

He punched in Jess's number.

5

Jessie Miller had just taken a window seat in Johnny's Bagels when her phone rang. She set her toasted garlic bagel filled with cream cheese and her coffee on the table.

She took the phone from her purse and saw it was Brian on the other end.

"You know, mailman, you spend way too much time on the phone. How will you ever get your route done like that, slacker?"

"Wow, I'm sure glad you aren't my boss, or I would be forced to quit my job and beg for money on the street." He heard her laughter.

She took a bite from her bagel and then asked, "What's up, Honey? We only spoke a little while ago."

"Carl called me and told me I didn't have to do a pivot, so I can definitely meet you for dinner. Of course, I'll have to have my snacks on the way to the food court. I can't resist all the different sauces and dips they sell there." He was happy because most pivots were one to two hours of helping another carrier finish his or her route. He especially disliked putting in OT in winter; darkness came much too early, making the job more difficult and sometimes hazardous.

"Oh, no. That means late night farts under the covers. I think I might have to move you to the sofa." She laughed again.

"Okay, I'll only have a couple samples and try to keep myself gas free."

"What time do you think you'll be able to meet me?"

"Probably around five, but I'll call if I'm going to be later. You know how the Post Office works. Eight and skate turns into staying out late. Okay, this slacker has to run. See you later."

He hung up before she could reply. There was something in the tone of his voice that bothered her, and she'd have to ask him about that later.

She looked through the glass and saw Sara McGinnis looking at her. She wasn't in uniform so maybe they could go shopping together. Jessie waved her in.

6

Sara strolled inside and when she came to the table, Jess stood up and gave her a big hug. They hadn't seen each other for a couple of months, and that was unacceptable because of what they both had gone through all those years ago.

"Sara, how are you? I hope everything is okay. You seem a bit distracted."

She took off her coat and hung it over the back of the chair. "I am, Jess. Mike made me take today off because of what happened yesterday." The waitress had come over, so Sara ordered coffee and a bagel.

"What happened?" Jess noticed that Sara's hands were trembling, and she kept clenching her fists.

The officer, wife of the new Chief of Police, stared deeply into her friend's eyes. "I was called to the scene of a domestic disturbance, and it was in *the* apartment. I had a great deal of difficulty going inside, even though I hadn't been there in eight years. I felt like I was stepping on my own grave."

As Sara prepared her coffee and bagel, Jess thought back to that day. When the police found out where the vampire was living, Sara had wanted to be the first one to raid the apartment, the apartment where she first, and unknowingly, made love with the vampire. She did not know she was involved with the monster who had killed four beautiful, young women since Black Friday, the day after Thanksgiving. Hard to believe that happened nine years ago."

"I understand perfectly how you feel. When I was abducted and taken to the Star of Bethlehem, full-well knowing that I could be that killer's final victim, I cringe every time I think about it, which is every Christmas season."

"Do you think we will ever get over that period in our lives?" Sara inquired. Her tremble had abated slightly, and she was able to pick up her coffee cup without spilling any on the table.

"Who knows? I've been hoping for a normal Christmas, but there is always a memory lurking somewhere." She heard Sara's phone ring.

"Hi, Honey," Sara answered, and after listening for a moment, she said, "I'm okay. I'm having coffee with Jessie and I think we might do some shopping together." A few moments later, she said, "'Bye, Mike. I'll see you later."

"Is he used to his new position yet, Sara?" Jess inquired.

"He's only been chief for two weeks, and he's really been working hard to get a handle on the job. He was only a lieutenant for a little less than two years before he accepted the appointment to chief. I'm sure that he will be okay once he learns all the nuts and bolts of the job."

7

Chief Michael P. McGinnis focused on the report he was reading, one of many that wound up on his desk every day. He'd only become chief a couple of weeks ago and was learning day after day the enormity of the position. The Bethlehem Police Department consisted of 154 officers and 40 civilians. The Patrol Division, led by a captain, consisted of four platoons, with a lieutenant heading each one, plus a traffic unit. There was also a Criminal Investigation Unit, and a Professional Standards Division.

As a lieutenant, he was only responsible for his platoon, which was a daunting enough task; but now his responsibilities seemed to be one-hundredfold of what it was during that part of his career, plus he still had to worry about Sara.

8

While Jessie was trying on some clothing she was interested in, Sara took a seat on one of the 'husband' chairs in the store and thought back to 2010. Hunting a vampire-the love of her life until she found out-was extremely taxing on both her body and her mind. There was certainly nothing in her police training that prepared her to deal with supernatural creatures, so they had to invent ways to try to subdue one.

A local author, Roy Clayton, had come up with a unique idea. Arrowheads would be made of glass and inside the glass and the hollow shaft of the arrow, Holy water would fill the empty space. When the arrow pierced the vampire's chest, the Holy water would be released inside the creature's body, hopefully killing it.

After the vampire was slain, she worked as a cop for a couple of months but then resigned. She came up with some ideas of what she would like to do for a living, and finally her love of art drew her to creating adult coloring books because of the new craze. Coloring was always relaxing when she was a kid, and she still had some coloring books that she worked in from time to time.

She was not enamored with the type of adult coloring books that were out because of the stained-glass type of pictures, so she created coloring pages of Historic Bethlehem buildings along with the modern ones that were popping up. She also created street scenes with figures in Colonial dress. Kids coloring books were fun, but she wanted to put more detail into her creations and make them more pencil friendly than crayons. Fine point markers would also work well for her pictures.

Sara also created hand-painted figurines that sold well but were extremely time-consuming to make. She sold these as special orders, not wanting to get into mass production.

Her business was doing extremely well, and she was making a good bit of money, but she missed being a street cop. She told Mike she was going to try to get reinstated; and after testing and revisiting the academy, she became a Bethlehem police officer on January 2nd, 2017. She had never regretted that decision, but yesterday, at the apartment, so many memories came back.

9

After Jessie decided what she wanted to buy, she took the items to the counter and paid. She noticed Sara sitting in a chair, her eyes having that 'thousand-yard stare' associated with combat vets and others that saw their 'elephant' in the jobs they did or the situations they were thrown into. Jess had her moments like that as well.

Instead of interrupting her friend's thoughts, she hung back and watched shoppers busily going about their business.

A couple of minutes later, she saw Sara come out of it and joined her friend to continue their shopping escapade.

They chatted incessantly as they walked, occasionally bumping into other shoppers who were swarming the streets, ducking in and out of stores, not paying attention to where they were walking as they texted on their phones. There were times that downtown Bethlehem was turned into complete chaos by non-residents looking for bargains in the best Christmas town in Pennsylvania according to a recent survey. The beauty of the city was enhanced by the famous Bethlehem streetlamps, the decorations, and Christmas music wafting from different stores.

Sara's eyes, seemingly always in cop mode, were in constant movement, scanning faces, doorways, and windows, focusing on anything that momentarily appeared out of place or unusual. She saw something that should not have appeared out of place, yet to her it was the proverbial 'elephant' in the room at this moment.

Jess said, "Let's take a look around *Cozy Capers*. Jim Blackman always has some great gift ideas."

Still keeping her eyes on the 'elephant', Sara replied. "I'll be in in a couple of minutes. I want to check something out first."

Jess saw what she was looking at, shook her head, and stepped into the store.

10

Jim Blackman was stocking shelves and listening to the *Osmond Family Christmas*. It had been one of his late wife, Jenna's, favorites, and he felt like her spirit was still with him, especially at Christmas time. Jim's mind wandered back to that time.

11

On Black Friday, 2010, Jenna Blackman was the first victim of the vampire. She had closed the store after an extremely profitable day. Attacked at her car, she was drained of blood, and the perpetrator of the crime was observed leaving the scene at an inhuman rate of speed. Patrolman Michael P. McGinnis rushed to the body and saw there was nothing that could be done to save her.

Three more beautiful young women were slain until the vampire was destroyed on Christmas Eve. The reign of terror was over, or so it was thought, until Christmas Day presented the Bethlehem Police Department with more supernatural creatures when two sets of large wolf tracks were found. The tracks were followed until they turned into human footprints. There were werewolves in the Christmas City.

12

He was brought out of it when he heard a voice say, "Hi, Jim. How are you?"

He stood up and saw Jessie Miller. He strolled over to her and gave her a big hug. "I'm doing pretty well, considering…"

She nodded, totally understanding where he was coming from. The two friends shared one of those lengthy moments when nothing had to be said. They both saw the 'elephant' and had suffered a certain degree of PTSD, dealing with it as best as they could, eight years later.

"So, what do you have new and exciting this year, Jim?"

"Step this way, young lady and I'll show you the really good stuff."

13

Sara fell in a couple of yards behind the man who looked *right,* yet he appeared *wrong.* She followed him into the parking deck of the *Hotel Bethlehem,* hanging back far enough that he couldn't see her.

He set the large, red cloth sack down behind his pickup truck and opened the tailgate. 'Santa', dressed for the part, took brown cardboard packages from the sack and tossed them into the covered bed of the truck as Sara eased closer, pulling her badge from her purse, telling him to turn around and face her.

"Santa, it looks like you have a pretty good gig going here. I assume you are a porch pirate, grabbing any and every parcel you can get your hands on and then just walk down the street, figuring that nobody would pay attention to a Santa carrying a sack full of presents. Very clever. We know there have been a ton of packages taken from porches, and it sure looks like you are one of the thieves. Ok, turn around now. I'm going to read you your rights and cuff you. I'll call for a nice, warm police car to take you to the station."

After her collar was transported away, she headed back to Cozy Capers and found Jessie still inside.

"Where have you been, Sara? Did your disappearance have anything to do with that Santa you were watching so closely?"

She nodded.

"Don't tell me you arrested Santa?"

Sara told Jessie and Jim what happened, and both were shaking their heads and laughing like there was no tomorrow.

Tomorrow's newspaper would feature a story about the Santa Claus package pirate.

14

Russ Gallagher, vice-president of *The Bethlehem News*, happened to see Sara McGinnis following Santa Claus. Santa was carrying a large, filled sack, and Russ's news antenna shot up. He smelled a story here. Grabbing his coat, he raced out of the office and began to follow them both, staying a discreet distance behind Sara. He knew Sara as a police officer and the wife of the new chief, Mike McGinnis.

As Sara made the arrest, Russ shot a video, capturing everything, to not only work into the story, but to protect Sara. She was not in uniform as she made the arrest.

Before Sara left the scene, after a patrol car came to pick up the prisoner, he got the man's name, Randall Burton. When Russ returned to the office, he did a Google search, finding that Burton had been arrested several times for shoplifting, public drunkenness, and previous package theft.

Last year Russ Gallagher had become a household name all around the world for revealing the existence of angels, Victoria Christmas, in particular. After his stories were filed, the readership of the small newspaper grew to numbers that could no longer be printed in the small office on Main Street. After building a new printing facility a few miles away, *The Bethlehem News* had the ability to print more than enough copies. The publisher and president, Alan Brossard, decided to suspend the online news service, encouraging readers to utilize the print service. Surprisingly, in a digital world, his foresight paid off. Every online reader immediately subscribed for home delivery of the newspaper.

After returning to the office, he sat at his desk and opened his laptop, writing the story titled *Porch Pirate Santa Arrested*

Yesterday, I was taking a short break from my job, looking out the window of our Main Street Office. Ever since moving here a year and a half ago, I have loved doing this, watching people going about their business, delivering to the many shops and restaurants, walking their dogs, darting in and out of shops, many carrying packages, and just enjoying the magic of downtown Bethlehem, the Christmas City.

I saw a Santa stroll by, at a fairly quick pace. Then a minute later my friend, Officer Sara McGinnis, walked by, keeping pace with the jolly old elf. Feeling there could be a story here, I grabbed my coat and headed down the street after them, keeping a distance between Sara and myself.

Our stroll ended in the parking deck of the Hotel Bethlehem where Santa set his filled-to-the-brim red sack on the macadam behind his pickup truck.

He opened the tail gate of the covered bed and began tossing the unwrapped, mainly brown boxes inside. I began videoing from my phone, stepping a little closer as Sara walked up behind him and announced her presence, showing him her badge. Santa was in a complete state of shock.

She arrested him and as she waited for a patrol unit to escort him the station, I approached them and asked Sara if I could question him.

"Certainly, Russ, but you know if you ask something that I don't want him to answer to a civilian, I'll have to shut you down."

"I understand, Sara."

Over the course of the few minutes, I found out his name, where he was from, and why he was stealing packages.

He told me his name was Randall Burton. He was a war veteran, now homeless, but he would not tell either of us why he was stealing packages, not even knowing what was inside the brown boxes.

"What in the world made you think that he was a thief, Sara?"

"As he was walking down the street, a handful of kids approached him, and he just brushed them off. I didn't think Santa would do that, and that's when I decided to follow him."

When I returned to the office, I did a Google search of him and found out he was indeed a war veteran, having served in Iraq, earning two Purple Hearts and a Sliver Star for a courageous act of saving two men from certain death.

I was looking forward to interviewing him in depth after he was booked and imprisoned or released. The question of why a homeless war veteran would steal packages needed to be answered.

15

After lunch, Russ took a stroll to the police station and asked if he could see Randall Burton.

Sergeant Vince Lorenz was behind the desk. He owed Russ a couple of favors and decided to stretch his authority just a little and allow the reporter access to the prisoner.

He was logged in and given a visitor pass. Officer Janet Morgan, a four-year veteran, escorted Russ back to an interview room, and after he stepped inside, she went to get Burton.

After escorting the prisoner to the interview room, she said, "Burton has not been seen by lawyer, so I am going to instruct him not to say anything to you that could be construed as privileged information unless he chooses to do so."

Officer Morgan had been instructed to stay with the two men to ensure that nothing out of hand would occur.

Russ re-introduced himself and sat down by the table. Burton followed suit.

"Randall, if I may call you by your first name?" He nodded so Russ continued. "When I was at my office, I did a Google search of you and found that you are an Iraq war veteran and a winner of the Silver Star along with two Purple Hearts for wounds received over there. Would you like to talk about it?"

Randall fidgeted, showing Russ that he was slightly uncomfortable, but he nodded his head. "That day was reminiscent to a World War One battle as both sides were entrenched, perhaps a hundred yards apart. Someone would raise his head far enough that the other side could see him, and then all hell broke loose for a couple of minutes. It went on like that for the better part of the afternoon; and as the sun began to set, two of our guys had had enough of it and began crawling across no-man's land, drawing a lot of fire but miraculously not getting hit. They were able to find a couple of old fighting holes and slithered into them.

"I knew both the guys pretty well, and I was so afraid that they were going to go home in bags for their recklessness. About a half hour later, a grenade landed in the one hole, and when it detonated, Specialist James Moore screamed that he was hit, but we didn't know how badly. PFC Richard Unger in the other hole exposed himself enough to empty a magazine toward the enemy, setting off another couple of mad minutes of rounds coming from their positions. I saw Rich spin around and fall backwards. Subsequently he was hit too, but again, how badly, was anybody's guess.

"Like an idiot, I started low crawling toward them, with rounds hitting very close to me, but I didn't get hit. I got to Rich first and saw he had taken a couple of rounds in his right shoulder and arm. He lost a lot of blood and was hovering between life and death, I figured. I couldn't let him die because he owed me almost three hundred bucks." He paused to see what kind of reaction he would get to this statement. I feigned surprise and then just nodded.

"As darkness set in, I pulled him back to our trench, and then I left to go back and get Jimmy. Jimmy was out of it, but he had a steady heartbeat. I moved my hands across his body and saw that his flak jacket had absorbed most of the shrapnel from the Iraqi grenade. I pulled him most of the way back and that's when I took a round in my right thigh and my left foot. That hit tore my boot completely off, and that's why I limp to this day. The next morning, a company of soldiers arrived, and they wiped out the Iraqis. We were able to get back to the basecamp. Jimmy and Rich both made it."

After hearing that story, Russ had to pause for a couple of moments to let it all sink in. He wanted to know more about this man. "Randall, that was an amazing story of courage. I can't even imagine what that could have been like. What can you tell me about your life before the military?"

16

By lunchtime, Brian Miller realized he would not be able to finish his route on time. Taking his break at Wawa, he called his supervisor to give him the bad news; but Brian was authorized to take as much time as needed to deliver all the mail. After he paid for his sandwich and soda, he went back out to his truck to eat inside 'the freezer on wheels'. Summertime lunches inside the Postal vehicle were like sitting in a sauna until he opened the door to catch whatever breeze might be available. He turned the truck on and waited for a little heat.

The call went straight to voicemail. "Honey, I'm not going to be able to have dinner with you at Christmasfest Market, but if you'd be okay with eating at Molly's or Mama Nina's, that would be good. If you choose Mama's, please bring a few beers along." Mama Nina's was a BYOB restaurant.

After finishing his meal and reading six pages in the novel he always carried, he drove to his first stop after lunch, scanning the barcode on the mailbox, signifying the official end to his lunch. He had scanned a barcode at Wawa, prior to getting his lunch, to show his supervisor- among others-that he was officially on lunch break. These two scans had to be performed within a one-half hour period. These were only two of myriad scans he would make during the day.

He went to the back of the truck, opened it and filled his satchel for the next loop of forty-three homes and two businesses. Along with a bundle of flats and two bundles of letter size mail, Brian placed four small parcels in the blue mailman's bag. He had one bundle of flats on his left arm, and a bundle of mail in his left hand. He would peel off the letters and flats for each stop. For his parcels, he used a turned around letter to show him where it was to be delivered.

After delivering the loop, including delivering a certified letter that had to be signed for, he returned to the truck. He put his satchel on top of the trays of mail still in the vehicle, placed all of the raw, outgoing mail, in a postal tub, and then closed the door.

As he walked to the right-hand driver's side of the FFV-flexible fuel vehicle, his phone rang. He unlocked the door and climbed in before he answered.

"Hi, Honey. What's up?"

"Oh my God, Brian, you will laugh so hard when I tell you what happened to Sara today. Yes, dinner at Molly's would be great. What time can you get there?"

"I think 6:30 should work. I want to take a shower and change at work before going out, unless you would prefer I come in uniform, then I could be there by 6:15."

"No, I'd rather you come in civvies. Six-thirty will be great."

"Super, see you then. Sara and Mike might join us, so you will be able to hear the story right from the horse's mouth."

"Can't wait. I haven't seen Mike since he took the job of police chief."

"K, see you later."

Brian drove two blocks to park for his next delivery loop.

17

Russ Gallagher was totally blown away by Randall Burton's life story, and he wanted to write it in a compassionate way. He sat down at his laptop, scrapping what he had already written.

Porch Pirate Santa's Plight

Yesterday, I was at my office window when I saw my friend Officer Sara McGinnis pursuing a man in a Santa suit carrying a filled red sack over his shoulder. Sensing a story, I followed them to the parking deck behind the Hotel Bethlehem.

Santa dropped his sack to the macadam and opened the tailgate of his pickup truck. He then proceeded to empty the sack into his truck. McGinnis approached him, announcing that she was a police officer, also flashing her badge.

I began to video the arrest on my phone, and asked Officer McGinnis if I could ask Santa some questions. While doing that, Sara looked though his bag and saw that the packages belonged to many people by the addresses on the packages.

He told me his name was Randall Burton and that he was a homeless, unemployed veteran. Later, I found out that he was an Iraq War army veteran and winner of two Purple Hearts and a Silver Star.

When I went to interview him at the Bethlehem Police Department, he told me how he won the medals. He saved two of his buddies from dying, and he is still in contact with them twenty-seven years after the battle. Both men are doing well, married with children, and a couple of grandkids on the way.

Born in Centralia, Pennsylvania, in 1960, Randall had a rough childhood and young adulthood. His father, a milkman, drank to excess, had affairs with women on his route, and abused both Randall and his mom constantly. When Randall was twelve, he found his dad's trunk in the attic and opened it to see what was inside. He rooted through old letters and pictures, an army uniform, and tchotchkes from his dad's childhood. At the very bottom of the trunk was a gun-actually a German Luger-that his dad must have taken from a dead enemy soldier. The gun was loaded, but Randall had no idea if it would work, having been in this trunk for nearly thirty years. He decided that if it worked, he would use it to end old dad's reign of terror. Randall was getting stronger but not nearly strong enough to take the old man on in hand-to-hand.

One day his dad came home, late as usual, and Randall was playing catch with his friend, Johnny Reardon. His dad, Sam, asked if he could play too. Randall wanted that very much, but when Sam had the ball, he threw a fastball strike that glanced off Randall's head. Had the teenager not moved quickly enough, the ball would have hit him in the right eye. Stunned, Randall wobbled to his bicycle and opened a saddlebag, pulling out the Luger. By now, old Sam picked up the ball and threw it as hard as he could into the small of Randall's back, dropping him to the grass. Randall writhed in pain as Johnny watched the elder Burton run toward his son, leaping into the air and crashing down on Randall's chest. Randall had the old Luger in his hand and fired it, hitting his father in the chest, killing him.

During the trial for the juvenile, testimony was given about how abusive Sam Burton was to both his wife and son. The jury concluded that Randall acted in self-defense, and the boy went free.

Good paying jobs were not very plentiful in Randall's area, eliciting him to enlist in the army after high school. He did so and excelled at the majority of physical and mental tasks he had to complete to graduate from Basic Combat Training. He then went to Fort Benning Infantry School, where he learned the art of becoming a sniper. He also trained in Special Forces. During his three years, he saw very little action, prompting him to get out and then join the French Foreign Legion.

By 1987 he had had enough of that life, resigned, and returned to Centralia, a town that was beginning to die because of underground coal fires that had been raging since 1962. The town was becoming a ghost town, but his mom and a few of her friends refused to get out. Randall stayed home to help her out for a couple of years, until her death in 1990.

He decided to re-enlist in the army, and he was finally able to use his special skills in Iraq in 1991. He stayed in the army for ten more years, getting out before 9-11. He was now forty-one and did not want to submit his body and mind to the rigors of war anymore.

Randall moved to Bethlehem in 2002 and got a job as a mail carrier, but he didn't like the work, nor the supervision, so he quit. Jobs were scarce, and he could not find a decent paying one. By 2016 he was out on the street, not able to afford an apartment. He filtered into the homeless community, bonding with ten to twelve veterans, and it was with these men and one woman that he began to steal from porches, trying to find items that his people could use to better their living conditions. If the box contained something for a child, he would return it under cover of darkness. He never took anything that was not useful to his 'community'. He would leave those unusable items in the Salvation Army bins.

Then he was arrested by Sara McGinnis.

As I listened to him share his life story, I totally believed everything he said. I will stand up for him at his trial because I feel he has suffered enough. I am setting up a GoFundMe page to help with his expenses, and I hope you will consider contributing and telling your friends about Randall Burton.

18

Brian saw Jessie, Sara and Mike sitting at a table, already enjoying a drink. After his day having to deal with sixty-three packages and a ton of mail, mostly Christmas cards, plus the joy of working in a cold rain most of his afternoon, he desperately needed one too. He strolled over and sat down.

The waitress, Alicia, a Moravian College student, strolled over to the table. Brian ordered a Goose Island IPA, and said, "When you bring my drink, I think we'll be ready to order. I know I'm starving, and I guess they are, as well."

"You got it, Brian."

He gave her a quizzical look. "You know me?"

"Yeah, you were my mailman a couple of years ago before you switched routes."

"Too many people to remember after all these years. Some of my co-workers have the knack of remembering thousands of names and a lot of faces. I just don't have that gift. Thanks for remembering me, though.",

When she walked away, Brian gave Sara a good, hard look.

She shrugged her shoulders and said, "What?"

"You *arrested* Santa Claus?" Just the way he said it propelled Mike to go into a laughing jag.

"Yeah, when I saw the report, I shook my head. Only *my* wife would arrest Santa, although he did deserve it."

After taking a couple of sips of beer, Brian said, "By the way, Mike. Congratulations on your promotion. You've come a long way, my friend."

"Thanks, Brian. I'm still learning, and I want to be a good chief. Now, back to porch piracy. I read an article in *The Morning Call* last week about the problem. With the number of packages stolen between Thanksgiving and

Christmas last year, one in twelve residences had packages taken from their porches. I've agreed to have a doorknob camera installed and dummy packages with GPS units inside them placed on my porch. We did that last Thursday, and so far they haven't been touched."

Sara interjected, "Honey, your name has been in the news quite a bit lately. Maybe people who commit these crimes, if there is a *gang*, have been told not to take anything from our house." Mike and her friends appeared curious by her statement, therefore she added, "Just saying."

Jessie defended her friend. "Sara could be right, guys," she offered.

A few minutes later, their plates arrived, and they heartily dug into some great Irish food, and listened to Christmas music from across the pond.

December 21st, 2018

1

Brian Kethledge's iPhone rang. He picked it up and looked at the time-1:27 AM, and the ID. "Hi, Julian. Have you finally arrived?"

"Yeah, there were a bunch of delays. I could have called for an Uber, you know."

Nonsense. I told you I would pick you up no matter what time you and Petra arrived. Did you bring Riley as I requested?"

"Of course, Doc," he replied, using his nickname from their time in Vietnam. "I've been telling him we are coming to see you; and every time I told him, he would jump up and down, bark like crazy, and spin around in circles. He has always been a crazy dog. I think he still misses Graeme, six years later, but they were together for so long..." His voice trailed off with emotion.

"Okay, I'll be there in about twenty minutes."

"Perfect. It will probably take that long to get Riley and our luggage."

"Good. I can't wait to catch up with you guys. Today will be kind of rough when we bury Sandy. I only wish it would have been her you could have saved, and not me."

"I know, but when an accident that bad, happens unless I would have been next to her, I wouldn't have been able to give her the gift. We'll talk when you pick us up."

2

Brian Kethledge enlisted in the army in 1966. After completing Basic Combat Training and Infantry Training, he volunteered to go through the Combat Medic Training at Fort Sam Houston, Texas. He learned how to deal with anything he would run into during his tour in the army. His training not only taught him how to take care of many types of wounds but also the treatment of animal, snake, and insect bites. Dehydration and heat stroke would be rampant in the jungles of Vietnam, and he learned how to make the men more comfortable if they experienced these maladies.

The following year he arrived in Vietnam where he was assigned to the 4th Infantry Division. He was taken to his company by helicopter, enjoying the cool air as it blew through the open doors. The scenery was magnificent, but down there in the paddies and jungles the enemy waited their arrival. Fortunately, the chopper took no fire, allowing the FNGs (effin' new guys) to acclimate themselves before getting shot at.

He was assigned to a platoon and met his platoon sergeant, Staff Sergeant Danny Roman, a gregarious young man who led his men through patrols with no KIAs for the first couple of months he was there. He knew that there would come a day that he would have men killed in action, but so far, they were damn lucky. Danny seemed to have a sixth sense when it came to contact with the Viet Cong and North Vietnamese Army units in the area.

Danny and Doc formed a very close bond during their time together until that day came that apparently ended Danny's life.

3

Months later, the understrength platoon had entered the jungle. Once they did, the sunlight became more diffused because of the density of the leaves. All the men searching for an unseen enemy, hoping not to find him, were having more and more difficulty seeing very far in front of them in the twilight-like conditions caused by the thickening vegetation. Above them was what was called triple canopy because the trees seemed to grow in three different sizes, each layer of leaves blocking out a little more light. The humidity became unbearable because all the heat was trapped between the soggy ground and the triple canopy. Slow and easy was the best course of action for the men. They walked this way for over an hour and then they heard the sound of rushing water. The water would cool them down and fill their nearly empty canteens. Doc smiled because every man would now be able to drink their fill and he wouldn't have to run short.

A couple of scouts went forward toward the sound and returned a few minutes later nodding their heads and smiling from ear to ear. No enemy was in sight, so they'd be able to take some time in the deep stream and then get on with the mission, refreshed.

As four guys kept watch, the rest of the platoon filled their canteens, adding purification tablets to kill most of the bacteria. After swishing the liquid around, it was safe to drink. When each man had enough, they all filled their canteens again, hoping the water would last until they'd settle in for the night.

While Doc and Danny were filling their canteens, side by side, splashing each other, laughing like hyenas, an enemy soldier with a great view of the stream from less than eighty yards away was the first of ten NVA to fire into the men frolicking in the water, their guards completely down; always a deadly mistake. The North Vietnamese Army often capitalized on American mistakes.

Danny hurried toward shore to grab his shotgun. He heard the round but there was absolutely no time to do anything. The heavy round caught him in the stomach, tearing through flesh and vital organs, exiting through his back. He knew he was dead as he fell into Doc's arms.

Doc realized there was nothing he could do, so he dropped his friend's body at the edge of the stream, and grabbed his M-14, firing and reloading as quickly as he could. He saw four or five men down and heard their screams. Killing the enemy became secondary; he needed to help his men and save their lives if possible.

He waded over to two soldiers and when he turned them over to see their faces, he knew they were gone. The next wounded soldier he came upon was shot in the shoulder. It was a through and through wound. He sprinkled the wound with sulfa powder and then placed a field dressing over the entrance and exit wounds. He had no morphine, so the soldier would have to bear the pain. After he finished, he patted the soldier on the shoulder. "Jake, you're going to be okay. Just hang in there until we can get out of this and get you back to the rear."

The firing had lessened some. The remainder of the platoon took cover behind the stream bank and were able to lay down enough suppressing fire to hear screams coming from the enemy line. A few minutes later there was total silence. That was the most eerie thing about a firefight. The calm only lasted a few brief moments until the wounded began to cry out again.

Doc patched up all the wounded as best as he could, and then he went to Danny's body. Closing his friend's eyes with his fingers, he said a quick prayer. Danny had no family and wasn't seeing anyone at the time; consequently, Doc didn't know what would become of his body. He decided he'd try to get him shipped to Bethlehem to be buried there. He'd escort the body if given permission to do so.

The platoon made their way from the stream and after checking the area where the NVA had been shooting at them, finding no bodies, but several blood trails, the LT ordered a short break. Those not wounded began to follow the trails while the injured remained with Doc and Dan's body, along with two healthy soldiers standing guard.

4

Six years ago, Brian and his wife Sandy were vacationing on Cape Cod, and they took a day trip to Martha's Vineyard. They had heard about the gingerbread houses and wanted to see the brightly painted small structures.

They walked through the circular community and stopped in front of one house that was the most brightly painted and saw the most amazing array of flowers and plants. Two men sat on the porch. The older man, wearing a kilt and missing a leg was talking to a younger man. A 3-legged dog slept on the porch between them.

After introductions, Brian and Sandy spent some time admiring Graeme's garden and petting Riley, while Brian studied the young man's face, certain that he knew him from somewhere. Later, on the ferry back to Cape Cod, he realized the man was actually his deceased platoon sergeant, Danny Roman. *How?* He still looked the same age that he was back in '67. The giveaway was the scar on his cheek.

After getting off the ferry, Brian took the car and followed the Hyannis shuttle bus. He saw Danny get off the bus and he kept out of sight until a young woman, Petra Ross, his wife, sat down at an outside table at the British Beer Company. Danny kept looking around and when he figured he wasn't being watched, he walked to the table and sat with his wife.

Moments later gunfire erupted, and Brian saw Petra take a round in the chest. Danny managed to take the two gunmen out, and the old Vietnam vet sprang into action. "Danny, get yourself and your woman in this car now."

They sped out of town and parked behind a closed lawn and garden shop.

5

Brian pulled up to the curb at Lehigh Valley International Airport. Julian had texted him, saying he, Petra, and Riley would be outside in about five minutes. The rain was coming down much harder now, but the temperature was quite mild. There was a possibility that today's high would break a record. He thought back to that day he first met them.

6

After he parked behind the garden center, Brian came around to the passenger side and opened the door, shoving Danny out of the way. He checked Petra's wounds. The round had gone clean through and it didn't appear as though any vital organs were punctured. "We're gonna have to get her to a hospital, Danny, or she won't make it. She's lost a lot of blood. I don't have anything with me to take care of her." Brian stared at him.

"Good to see you again, Doc. It's been a long time."

"Yeah, it has, but we can go over all that once we get her out of danger."

"Don't worry, Doc. My blood will save her life." He took out a knife and sliced through his right palm. Opening her mouth, he forced his blood into her mouth and on her tongue. She swallowed. He repeated the process two more times and then said, "Come on outside, Doc. This will take an hour or so, but she'll be fine. The wound will heal and then she'll be like me."

Brian looked shocked. "And what might that be Danny?"

He sighed. "I am immortal and that's why certain people are hunting me down. I thought I was off the radar these past ten years or so, but they caught up with me. I guess I have a lot to tell you. How did you know it was me after forty-eight years?"

Brian slid down the side of his car and sat down hard on the ground. He looked into his eyes. "It's hard to forget someone who dies in your arms, Danny. Your face has been haunting me ever since that day."

Danny took a seat on the ground next to his old friend. "I wanted to tell you that I was immortal and that if I would die, I would come back to life, but I just didn't want to put you in a position where someday people might come after you because you knew my secret."

Brian nodded his head. "I guess I can understand that, but your disappearance has been gnawing in my gut for all these years. After you vanished, one of the soldiers standing guard came over to me and told me your body was missing. While the two wounded soldiers rested, two other guys and I swept the jungle about fifty meters out from our break area. I found your boot prints, but I knew that dead men did not get up and walk away." He stood up and began pacing, looking in at Petra waiting to see when she would rise from near death, her body completely healed. "When we returned to the wounded men, I instructed everybody to say that your body was pulled away by a tiger. I told them that if we told the LT and the other men the truth, they would think we all cracked under the strain of combat and they'd put us in a rubber room for the rest of our lives. Danny, where did you go?"

The immortal stood up, placing a hand on Doc's shoulder. "I haven't been Danny in a long time, Doc. For most of my lives, I have been Julian Ross." Doc nodded, and Julian continued. "I came back to life, and I saw you tending to the two wounded guys. Since the guards were looking toward you and not me, I quietly got up and walked away into the jungle. I roamed around for several days and wound up in a Vietnamese village. I gave an old papasan a thousand piasters to get me to Quin Nhon. I lived underground with the AWOLs and deserters for a couple of weeks and then I managed to hop a flight back to *The World*, posing as a civilian. Graeme had created some good papers and sent them to the American Embassy in Saigon. I simply strolled in and identified myself and asked if a package had arrived for me. The clerk handed it to me with no questions asked. A week later I was back home."

7

Brian smiled as he saw his friends stroll out of the airport.

Julian let go of Riley's leash and the dog raced toward Brian, jumping high off the concrete, giving him a lick every time he jumped high enough. Shortly after the immortals had moved to Seattle, Julian found out that he could have a prosthetic leg made for Riley, and he jumped at the chance. Riley got used to it rapidly, but when he and Sandy visited them, Brian noticed that Riley sniffed at it a lot. He always wondered what that amazing little dog was thinking. Perhaps someday in his long, long life to come, science would come up with a way to make animals speak.

Petra ran to Brian, hugging him and kissing him. "God, Doc, it is so good to see you. You haven't aged a day in 5 years."

A tear fell down his cheek. "I know. I wish Julian would have been here to be able to give Sandy the gift, and then I wouldn't have to go through eternity alone."

"Doc, Sandy can never be replaced, but you know you will always have us." She whispered, "Julian is going to try to convince you to come back to Seattle with us, and then his new 'Family' will be together again."

Into her ear he softly said, "I will think about it."

Suddenly they were wrapped by two strong arms. "Man, it is so good to see you, Brian. We have a lot to talk about."

When they crossed the Hill to Hill Bridge, Julian said, "The Star of Bethlehem is really bright."

Brian noticed the star and laughed. "I guess this is miracle number one for this Christmas season."

Petra interjected, "Seeing this star is a miracle? How is that, Brian?"

"The hours the star is lit are from sunset to midnight. I have no idea why it is lit right now, but I imagine that if others see it, there will be a lot of phone calls and probably pictures taken of it as well. Last year, several miracles occurred in the city because Bethlehem was visited by a tried and true, dyed in the wool angel. Her name was Victoria Christmas and her story was written by Russ Gallagher, who had only been working at the *Bethlehem News* for six months. His wife Joanne had been paralyzed for several years, but on Christmas Eve she was healed. It was a pretty amazing time.

"I would certainly guess that attaining immortality would be considered a miracle," Brian said.

Although the motions were unseen, Petra and Julian nodded

Julian said, "I met the man, who would give me the gift in 1773. Joshua Bennet strolled onto our farm and my father offered him a job. It was my task to teach him all about farming, and it didn't take long before we became friends. Two years later, against the advice of my father, Joshua and I joined the Continental Army.

"Fighting side by side was a great service to the many who wanted a free America and, although there were many difficult times, we persevered. My lowest point occurred in December of 1779, when we arrived at our winter encampment at Jockey Hollow, near Morristown, New Jersey. I had been wounded in the leg in September and I had to use my rifle as a crutch many times in order to keep moving forward.

"Joshua cared for me, as I reached my lowest point. I feared that in order to live my leg would have to be removed, and I didn't know if I could make that decision. Joshua applied an ointment to my leg several times a day, and I received my first miracle when the wound healed, and I was able to walk. At the time I didn't know that Joshua sliced his hand and rubbed his blood all over my wound.

"When I was fully recovered, he and I had a long talk and he told me his story. He was born in 1474 to a wealthy family in Spain. As he matured, he learned many things, including several languages, mathematics, astronomy, physics, and geometry. He joined the Spanish army and fought the Moors. Several years later, he joined Columbus on his second voyage to the New World, enjoying the life of a seafarer. However, he needed to go back to crush a rebellion before he could set out on his own.

"Finally, in 1513 he was able to set off to sea to search for new lands and riches for Spain. He landed in

Florida. Although he did not know it at that time, he discovered the elixir that afforded him immortality.

"Eight years later, he went to Spain and recruited people to join him in Florida. He then returned to Florida with two ships, bringing over two hundred people including priests, farmers, and artisans to colonize the land, but they were attacked by native American warriors, and he died in San Juan, Cuba, where he was entombed. After coming back to life, it took some time to escape from the tomb. He hid a short distance away and watched until two people found his body was missing.

"At that time no one would have ever considered proclaiming that he was missing. When his 'body' was transferred to the Cathedral of San Juan Bautista, he was there to witness the event.

"Over the years he traveled wherever he felt like going to and stayed for ten to twelve years if he really liked the locale he chose. He often ventured back to Florida and kept to his ten to twelve-year schedule. He moved around the country, enjoying the new, untamed places he found.

"His real name was Ponce De Leon."

A thick silence permeated the interior of the car.

Brian drove down Broad Street and after a couple of turns, he traversed Market Street until coming to his beautiful historic home a couple of blocks from Main.

All the white Christmas lights were turned on, and every window held an electric candle.

"Brian, this is absolutely gorgeous," Petra stated.

"Thanks. We bought it several years ago. Sandy had been in love with this house since she was a little girl, and when it came up for sale, we jumped all over it. Making sure we were the highest bidder, we added twenty thousand to what we thought we would need to offer. Fortunately, we outbid a couple by forty-five thousand dollars."

Stepping inside, the warmth of gas heat along with the scent of pine, had everyone taking off their coats shortly after stepping inside. Next to the door were six hooks screwed into the bottom of a small mantle that held two bayberry candles. Although they were not lit, Julian and Petra could smell them.

"If you guys want to head to bed, your room is upstairs, second door on the right. I haven't slept since the accident, and I think I'm going to have a beer and make a sandwich."

"Doc, we're immortals, remember. We don't need to sleep. Besides, a beer and a sandwich sounds perfect," Petra said, giving the older man a hug.

"What she said, Doc. I'll just take our luggage up and then we'll hang out and talk."

"Thanks, guys. I sure could use some human company." The sirens of a couple of emergency vehicles could be heard and the red lights seen as they passed by.

8

Five minutes later a phone rang in another part of town.

"McGinnis," the groggy man said as his wife also sat up and turned on her light.

He listened for a short period of time and then replied, "I'll be there in fifteen."

"What happened, honey?" Sara McGinnis inquired as her husband got off the bed and began getting dressed.

"Two of our cops were in a high-speed chase with a drunk driver, and there was an accident. Bruce Davidson was killed, and Connie Abernathy is badly injured. The firemen on the scene are trying to get her out of the vehicle with the Jaws of Life. I'm afraid that if she doesn't get to the hospital soon, she won't make it."

"Give me a call when you find out anything."

"I will. Go back to sleep."

9

Petra was in the kitchen helping Brian make sandwiches. He had taken two bowls from the cupboard, filling one with the dry dogfood he purchased yesterday after calling Julian and the other with cool water from the sink.

Riley was jumping around in anticipation of a meal until Brian set the dishes on the floor and patted him on the head.

They took the food and beers into the living room just as Julian bounded down the steps.

The three immortals sat down in comfortable chairs, facing the fireplace. The warmth felt good. Brian said, "Sorry it's not a real fireplace, but Sandy and I decided to convert it to gas to eliminate the mess of dealing with wood, sparks, and soot. Gas is just so clean and even."

"It is still really pretty to look at, Brian," Petra replied. "Also, you and Sandy decorated the place quite nicely." Spread out throughout the room were Clothtique Santas, Beyer's Carolers, and hand painted Pipkas. Sandy had laced the collectibles with greens, berries, and small candles.

Brian smiled. "She always had the gift. I'd bring all the tubs, boxes and bags up from the basement, and then Sandy would work her magic. She'd decorate one room at a time, not continuing until she thought every item was placed perfectly. I used to move decorations around when she was not in the room, and she would yell and laugh at me all at the same time...." He began to cry. "I really miss her, and I will miss her for a very long time."

His iPhone rang. When he pulled it from his pocket, the ID said 'Mike'. "Mike, what in God's name are you calling me at two-thirty in the morning for? You're too young to have insomnia." Brian laughed at his own joke.

Brian listened without interrupting and about a minute later he ended the call without even responding. His eyes were streaming tears, and his voice was cracking when he spoke to his friends. Riley, sensing he needed a friend, got up from his spot in front of the fireplace, walked over to Brian and placed his snout on Brian's legs. Brian smiled and automatically began to pet him, saying, "Ri, I don't know how you know, but you always come to me at the right time. That was Mike McGinnis, my police officer friend. Actually, a couple of weeks ago he became the chief, one of the youngest ever in the city. Sandy's best friend, Connie, a police officer who is planning to retire at the end of the year, was in a horrible accident earlier. It must have happened just before we heard the sirens. She and her partner were in a high-speed pursuit of a drunk driver who fired shots at them from the driver's side window. The two cars crashed, and Officer Bruce Davidson was killed instantly. He just became a father in October. They're working on getting Connie out of the car, and if she doesn't get to a hospital soon, she might not make it."

"Doc, you know I can help her if I can get to her in time."

"I know, Julian. Sandy had been telling me for a long time that if anything would ever happen to her, I should get together with Connie and marry her. She is a lot of fun to be with. The accident scene is only about five blocks away. Let's go and see if you can save her. Mike knows about us, so there would be no problem getting you to the car."

10

Less than five minutes later, the three immortals arrived at the scene. They left Riley behind to guard the house and probably finish eating the remaining sandwiches.

Brian had called Mike just before leaving the house, and when the chief saw his car, he hurried over to talk to his friend.

"Mike, this is Julian Ross and his wife, Petra. If there is any chance he can get to her, he can still save her."

While shaking Julian's hand, Mike said, "Yeah, I can get you to the car, but you're going to have to be really discreet, or the fire men and women will learn something that I'm sure you don't want them to know."

Mike walked Julian to the car, and he could see Connie inside. She was losing a lot of blood, and Julian was certain she would never make it to a hospital. "My blood type does not matter, because immortal blood can be accepted by anyone," he whispered.

"Ok, let's do it," Mike decided.

"Firemen and women, this man has type O blood and he is a doctor. He doesn't think Officer Abernathy can survive much longer without getting a transfusion while you are trying to get her out of the vehicle." Suddenly, Lydia Owens, a five-year veteran of the BFD yelled. "We cracked the roof and we can get her out."

They pulled her from the vehicle and after she was placed in the back of the ambulance, the paramedics went to work on setting up for the transfusion. Moments later the ambulance was on the way to St. Luke's Hospital, with Julian's life-saving blood flowing into Connie Abernathy's arm. He smiled because his *family* had now grown to five.

11

The immortals sat in Connie's room, drinking lousy hospital coffee, waiting for her to awaken. Julian sensed that it would not be too much longer before she breathed her first immortal breath.

She opened her eyes and stared at the two strangers, and then softened her glance when she saw Brian. "I felt like I was hit by a truck, but now I feel wonderful. What happened?"

Brian stood up and stepped to her bedside. "Connie, you were in a terrible accident and many people there didn't think you would make it. This man," he said, pointing to Julian, "saved your life by giving you a transfusion of his blood. Please don't be angry, but now you are like us. You are immortal."

Letting that statement soak into her groggy brain for a few moments, she finally smiled. "I am glad to be alive, even if it will be forever. Brian, as long as you are here for me and with me, it's all good. Sandy would have wanted us to be together."

After officially introducing her to Julian and Petra, she began to ask many questions and the other three immortals would take the time to answer every one.

12

Bethlehem was awakening. There were only four shopping days until Christmas, and soon store owners, or employees, would be opening their doors, waiting for the hopeful onslaught of customers. These next four days would make or break several of the shops on Main Street.

One of those stores on the cusp was *Retro*, a shop that specialized in used records, used books, trading cards, and toys and gifts from the forties to the sixties. They had a great run the first year they were open, but the past two years the owners were barely keeping their heads above water. A similar store in a suburb of Chicago had recently gone out of business, and *Retro* bought their inventory, sight unseen, for six cents on the dollar. Lon and Al Seager, Vietnam vet brothers, were expecting the shipment today, hoping the nine-thousand-dollar investment would pay off.

A few minutes later a tractor trailer pulled up on Main Street. The brothers, the driver, and his helper began to unload the forty-foot trailer filled with boxes of items, and they stacked the boxes in the near empty storage room. When all the boxes were off the truck, it departed, and the brothers began to rummage through their purchases. The first boxes they opened contained hula hoops; and when all those boxes were opened, they found over one thousand of the round, plastic playthings. Lon had an idea and shared it with his brother who smiled and nodded.

Although they wouldn't open many boxes until well after Christmas, they would find several rare, valuable items including three sealed copies of the Beatles *Yesterday and Today* album-the butcher cover version, which they would sell for nearly seventy-thousand dollars to a collector. Other items in the boxes would eventually be sold for almost nine hundred thousand dollars, but the pièce de résistance was a T206 Honus Wagner baseball card inside a sealed plastic case that would fetch almost three million dollars at an auction early in 2019. They would also find many toys and games that were out of production for up to seventy years, and over time customers would pay large sums of money to have one or more of these pieces of their childhoods.

13

Jessica Weida, manager of the *Moravian Book Shop,* and three employees were stocking the shelves with new books and preparing a table for their author of the day. Sherrl Wilhide was a local waitress who finally penned her first book *Waitressing and Werewolves.* She was still a waitress at the famous *Brass Rail* restaurant in Allentown, and three years ago she was the only civilian to anyone's knowledge who had ever slain a werewolf. The chuckle factor of the anecdotes was a ten for sure, and her book was making a steady climb up the *New York Times* bestseller list. She would be signing copies today from 1 to 4.

Moravian Book Shop, the oldest continually operating bookstore in the United States, and possibly the world, had been facing possible closure. Owned by the *Central Moravian Church,* it was no longer profitable for the church to keep operating the store hence they sold it to Moravian College, which needed a larger bookstore for the students.

It opened in 1745, but there were changes over the next two-hundred and seventy-three years. The bookshop moved to Arch Street, in Philadelphia, but returned to Bethlehem two years later in 1858. In 1871, the store moved to its present location where the church housed its publishing facility.

14

Gwen Richards was busily setting a table for four in the 1741 The Terrace dining room of the Hotel Bethlehem. Guests would not be arriving until the dinner hour. The Tap Room was open for lunch, and as she prepared the restaurant, she was also waitressing The Tap Room. Signed photographs of many of the celebrities who had stayed in the hotel, or eaten there, graced the walls of the Tap Room. She loved keeping busy, especially now that she only worked here over her fall break and summer vacation. She began her studies to obtain her bachelor's degree at Millersville University four months ago.

Last year she had been saddled with debt. Her mother's medical bills were outrageous, and she didn't know if she would ever be able to live her dream of being an oncology doctor without running up a debt that she would unlikely be able to repay.

She was waitressing at two places to help keep her mother comfortable, and until mom passed, or was able to go to a care facility, she would not be able to take classes anywhere.

Gwen brought the check to her two guests, Craig Murphy and Russell Gallagher. During the time they had a couple of drinks and then dinner, Craig Murphy told Gallagher, the reporter, his story.

He had won 317 million dollars, and it was his mission to give it all away to help people in need before he passed.

When Gwen handed Craig the check, he handed her one for the total of two hundred and seventy-three thousand dollars to use to pay off her mother's medical expenses, four years of college, and four years of medical school. Along with the check was an investment option to help her money grow. She gave him a hug and paid off their debts in a short amount of time.

She was called over to the Tap Room to take care of a guest and saw Russ Gallagher seated at the table. Gwen gave him a hug and sat down with him to chat for a moment.

"Mr. Gallagher, how nice to see you again. How are you?"

"I'm wonderful and Joanne is also doing well, but I want to know how you are."

"Thanks to Mr. Murphy, everything is going so well. I've been able to keep up with my mom's medical expenses. I have invested almost two hundred thousand dollars and I am getting nice dividends for my investment. I've just finished my first semester at Millersville with a 4.0 grade average.

"That is wonderful. One of the suits is giving you the evil eye, so I guess you should get up and take my order. I really would like to get together with you while you're home and talk."

She stood up and took his order. "Absolutely. I'll be home till the second week of January, although I have a pretty full schedule here. Give me your card, and I'll email you when I know I'll be free."

"That would be great." He handed her his card."

She looked at it and nodded. "VP of the paper. That's very cool." She sauntered off to get his drink.

15

Across the street, Lon and Al were on the sidewalk outside the store, in the rain, hula hooping to classic Christmas music, telling passersby, "Win $500 in merchandise by out-hula hooping your competitors. Last participant standing will win this gift tomorrow. Buy a hula hoop for only seven dollars, go home and practice, and come back tomorrow at 2 PM." During the remainder of the day, and Saturday morning, they would sell four hundred hula hoops. However, not everyone who purchased would participate.

The challenge was put out on Facebook and was shared ninety-one times on Friday.

Lon asked Chief McGinnis if they could close the Main Street Bridge for a half hour tomorrow for the contest. McGinnis thought about how much inconvenience it could cause drivers, but he thought the contest would be quite fun. He decided to authorize the time to the store owners, mainly because of their service to the country, and he'd deal with the backlash when it came in. He would have signage announcing the closure placed by the bridge entrance on Route 378 within the hour. During the contest, Lon and Al's wives and kids would watch the store while their husbands played on the bridge. They would make a huge donation to the Police Athletic League in 2019.

16

Sherrl Wilhide took a seat behind the table set up for her book signing. This was not only her first book, but the first time she would be signing for total strangers, mixed in among her friends and fans. Sherrl was a self-published author, therefore, she brought copies with her. She only brought fifty books, and she figured that was more than enough. By three o'clock she only had thirteen copies left and thought she might have to end her signing early. She was amazed with the turnout, and if she would run out, she'd take their names and addresses and would send them their books as quickly as possible.

During a short downtime period, she thought back to that day almost three years ago when she killed a real live werewolf.

17

She was visiting her friend, Samantha Stewart, who lived in a beautiful home less than a couple of hundred yards south of South Mountain.

After settling in and then shopping in downtown Bethlehem, they returned to the house for dinner, TV and girl talk. Sam had stepped away from the table to take a call. The TV was on, and Sherrl was afforded a view of the screen from her place at the table. Suddenly the words 'Special Report' took over the screen, and a moment later she heard the words of a local reporter talking about werewolves escaping from a secret research facility inside South Mountain. Five years earlier, she had been scared when the vampire reports kept coming from Bethlehem and she was not going to shrug this off as a prank. She believed it with all her heart.

After her friend ended her phone call, Sherrl said, "Sam, I just heard a report on WFMZ that there were werewolves running around in this area, and I am frightened like crazy. What do we do if one or more of them break into the house?"

"I don't know, Sherrl. Should we turn off the lights and hide somewhere?"

"Where would we hide? I would think that a werewolf would be able to smell us no matter where we hunkered down. Do you have anything made of solid silver? In all the movies I've ever seen and the books I've read a werewolf can be killed with something silver piercing its heart."

"The fireplace pokers are silver, and I have some large knives that are solid silver, but how could we get close enough to kill these creatures?" The fear in her voice seeped out like syrup from a bottle.

"I think we better turn off all the lights and just hang out here. The odds of a werewolf coming to our door, huffing and puffing, must be higher than buying a winning lottery ticket. I'll go turn off the outside light and you get the inside ones." She walked to the front door and had her finger on the switch ready to flip it off when she saw a large shadow cross the windowpanes. Shivering, she quickly turned off the light and gazed out into the night. When she saw nothing was there, she calmed down and strolled back into the living room as a hairy face with large yellow eyes peered into the house, seeing the two women.

The wolf crashed through the large front window, growling and spitting saliva, heading right toward Sherrl. Sam saw the beast and screamed loud enough that the neighbor across the street heard her. He had just stepped outside for a smoke.

Sherrl turned toward the creature and quickly dove to the floor as the werewolf leaped over where she had just stood. She wound up in front of the fireplace, feeling the warm glow thrown off by the burning logs, and grabbed the silver tipped poker and the silver shovel as well.

The wolf had leaped so far that it crashed into the dining room table, causing wine glasses and plates to fly. The table splintered when the animal hit it with all its force and it was just enough to stop its momentum, giving Sherrl the precious seconds she needed to prepare for a life and death fight. She prayed harder than she had ever prayed before, and when the wolf got back on its feet, turning toward Sam who was cowering in a corner of the large room, Sherrl knew it was now or never. She charged the large animal, thrusting the point of the poker into its side as hard as she could and then she wielded the shovel like a sword and took a swipe at the wolf's neck, partially severing it from its body. The wolf howled in pain, its eyes now cloudy as Sherrl withdrew the poker from it and stabbed it where she thought its heart would be.

Long moments passed as the wolf writhed and howled, finally falling to the floor in a pool of blood, dead.

The adrenaline was beginning to wear off and Sherrl collapsed in a heap, while Sam raced to her aid.

Several neighbors, who heard the howling and screaming, were now gathered just inside the door, staring at the gruesome action with their mouths wide open, although two or three had the presence of mind to call 911. They had also been alerted by all the dogs in the neighborhood who were barking and howling.

18

She came out of her reverie when she heard a voice crying out, "Earth to Sherrl, earth to Sherrl. Are you still with us?"

She saw her old friend Samantha Stewart standing in front of her table, a wide smile plastered on her face. She had neither seen, nor heard from her old friend since that day three years ago, and she knew they had a lot of catching up to do.

The author stood up and walked around the table to give her old friend a huge hug and a kiss, almost on the lips. "Sam, it is so good to see you. You know I have about a thousand questions to throw out at you."

"I know. As Ricky Ricardo would have said, "Lucy, you have a lot of 'splaining to do."

Releasing her friend, Sherrl said, "I'll be finished here in less than a half an hour. How about we have a late lunch and a couple of drinks at The Tap Room?"

"That would be great. I need to put more money in the meter, and then I'll meet you there. I have missed you so much."

"Me too, girlfriend. See you in a little bit," she said, as a customer stopped by her table.

At four o'clock, Jessica Weida came to the table to talk to Sherrl. "Wow, Sherrl, you have had an amazing day. I must admit I have not read your entire book, but some of the anecdotes about waitressing had me both laughing and crying. I well know, as a customer service representative how insanely demanding buyers can be at times. I've actually been compiling some things that people have said in a journal. Who knows, perhaps someday I will write a similar type of book. Of course, I fervently hope that it will not include a section about werewolves, vampires, or whatever. I look forward to working with you again." She shook Sherrl's hand and went back behind the counter.

19

The Tap Room at the *Hotel Bethlehem* was packed. Happy Hour began at three and would continue until six-thirty. Sherrl looked around and saw Sam wave to her from a table for four next to a window. There were two people seated with her and, at a glance, Sherrl did not recognize them.

After working her way through the crowd, she arrived at the table, and then recognition set in. The man and the woman, both in their late sixties, nodded to her and then they shook hands.

When Sam introduced her to the couple, they both said, "So nice to meet you, Sherrl."

"No, it is my pleasure to meet you. Your music has given me great joy for a long time. Are you in Bethlehem to perform somewhere?"

"Yes. We're just performing to a small crowd tonight at *Godfrey Daniels*. After being out of the limelight for the past decade, we wanted to start out at a small venue. Our friend, Peter, told us about the place and he said he always enjoyed playing there after he went solo from his band," the man said.

"So, how do you guys know Sam?"

Drinks were placed on the table by a waitress named Gwen.

The woman replied, "When we were kids, Sam and her folks were our neighbors. When we were teenagers, we were awarded our first record contract, and the promoters wanted us to go out on the road as soon as we could. There were several brother and sister acts appearing across the country, and we had a pretty good little club act going. We were writing our own material and figured that we would have enough songs for two future albums. I Googled brother and sister duos, and there are more than I would have ever thought..." Her attention was diverted to a sight across the street. "Look at that."

The foursome looked out the window and saw about twenty-five to thirty people of all ages playing with hula hoops outside *Retro*. Some of the participants were very good, and as they watched for several minutes, more people came from the store carrying their new toys, ready to join the group.

Sam said, "I wonder what that is all about?"

When Gwen brought another round of drinks, she saw the hoopers. "I heard that tomorrow they are closing down the Main Street Bridge for a hula hoop contest. The winner is going to receive a five-hundred-dollar shopping spree at *Retro*. I think I'm going to get one later and give the contest a shot. It looks like a lot of fun." She left their table to serve others.

"Okay, back to the story," the man said. "We were precursors to *The Carpenters* by about three years, except in reverse. She plays piano and I am the drummer. We usually travel with a guitarist and a bass player who also sing. They were with us in the beginning, but after I was drafted, the group had to break up, and we didn't hook up with them again until years later. They are actually over at the venue getting everything ready." He looked at his watch. "Sorry folks, but we have to get going in order to have a little time to rehearse. I wish I could give you guys free tickets, but the concert is sold out."

They stood up and shook hands, stepping outside to a waiting limo.

20

"Wow, Sam. Meeting Jenny and Gerry was one of the coolest things that has ever happened to me. I wish we could go to see them. Perhaps there will be another time in the near future."

"Possibly. Actually, they were very excited about meeting you. They bought your book last month on *Amazon* and were quite bummed out leaving the copy in their hotel room. They wanted you to sign it. Neither of them could believe that a little bitty woman like you could be able to kill a werewolf and live to tell about it. And that is what I want to talk to you about.

"Sherrl, I've lived with my shame of not helping you engage that beast. After it was over, I was so upset that I moved a couple of days later and didn't want to talk to you. You could have been killed, and I was unable to pitch in and do my part to eradicate that creature."

"Honey, it's okay. Gosh, it happened so fast. I don't pray a lot, but in those few terrifying minutes God got an earful, and I've been thanking Him every day since for allowing me to live. I had to tackle the werewolf, because I didn't want you to die. I would have never been able to live with myself if that would have happened. I wish you would have talked to me, and then, maybe we wouldn't have missed three years of drinking, carousing, and lots of talking."

Sam was crying, and no words would come to her. She probably would have choked the words back trying to talk in this state. Her friend was not angry. Now she was upset for the three years of being apart. She would make it up to Sherrl, starting right now.

"Sherrl, would you like to stay here and have dinner? Chances are we'll have to stay put at this table, but I want to check to see if we can get a table in the Terrace."

"Sam, this is absolutely fine. Please don't attempt to get another table. Besides, in the Terrace we wouldn't be able to see the crowd playing with hula hoops." By now the number of participants had swelled to close to one hundred people. They were blocking the street, but nobody seemed to care until two police cars showed up, and in five minutes the cops had dispersed the gathering crowd and the hula hooping fanatics.

21

Russ and Joanne Gallagher saw the people and had to see what was going on firsthand. They walked down the street from the newspaper office. Joanne stepped into *Retro*, strolling back outside with a hula hoop of her own. She put it around her waist, holding on to it, and then gave it a spin, allowing her body to work in a circular motion, keeping the hula hoop around her waist, continuing to pick up speed. That worked for about a minute and then the red and white striped hoop fell to the sidewalk. She repeated these movements several times and finally was rewarded with keeping the hula hoop moving around her waist for five minutes before it fell again.

She raced to her husband, laughing loudly. "I did it, honey. That was so much fun." As he had watched her, he was so happy. It was not even a year ago, that she was confined to a wheelchair, her spine paralyzed from an automobile accident over three years ago.

They walked, hand in hand, to the *Hotel Bethlehem.* The odds of waiting less than an hour for a table were slim to none, but they had nothing but time. Stepping through the front door, Joanne set her hula hoop against the wall near the umbrella stand, a well-used item today.

They walked to the hostess and were told that the wait would be an hour and fifteen minutes. While Joanne grabbed a comfortable chair in the lobby, Russ stepped to the bar to get them each a drink. The Christmas spirit was in full bloom with music playing, people talking and having fun, some gifts being exchanged, and just an overall good feeling of joy. Since last year, Russ knew that he would love Christmas more and more every day. There were still times that he thought he'd caught a glimpse of Victoria Christmas, but the angel was probably very busy helping people on another part of the planet.

He got his drinks and was rewarded when a man got out of his chair next to Joanne, giving him a seat until dinner. He looked across from him and saw the smiling face of a rival reporter from *The Morning Call* Bethlehem office. He lifted his glass to Nicole Mertz.

"HI, Nicole. How are you? I read your article, *This Is Bethlehem,* this morning, and it was a wonderful piece." Looking toward his wife, he added, "This is my wife, Joanne."

"Joanne, what a pleasure. Yours is one of the most miraculous stories ever written. I can't even imagine what it could be like being touched by the hand of an angel."

"What was your article about, Nicole?"

"On Christmas Eve, from dusk until sunrise on Wednesday, the word 'Hotel' on top of this building will go dark leaving only the word Bethlehem, in neon red. It was a tradition from back in the '70s to pay homage to the birth of Bethlehem. I don't know if you know it, but the hotel stands roughly where the First House was built when the Moravian missionaries settled here 277 years ago." Joanne shook her head.

"The leader of the settlers, Count Nicholas Ludwig von Zinzendorf, celebrated Christmas Eve with them in that log structure with a wall separating them from their animals. Because the building was reminiscent of the stable where Jesus was born, he decided to name the settlement Bethlehem.

"Bruce Haines, managing partner of the *Hotel Bethlehem,* was notified of the tradition by Debbie Helms, who was a hotel employee from 1972 to 1990. She told him she recalled the tradition while walking to choir practice at the Central Moravian Church one evening. She told him that by turning off the 'Hotel' part of the sign, it was transformed from being an advertisement to showing the location of the city, a place where people could enjoy the holidays. 'Bethlehem,' Debbie said, 'has so many beloved holiday sights-single candles in the windows and, of course, the Bethlehem Star. The sign was another one that simply lost traction over the years.' She didn't recall the tradition continuing in the 80s."

"That is a great story, Nicole."

"Thanks. I have to go now; my table is ready. It was a pleasure talking to you both and have a very Merry Christmas and a Happy New Year."

22

As the evening wore on, fewer shoppers were strolling the sidewalks. Many of the stores would be closed by eight. Money was now being spent in restaurants and bars, patrons winding down their days. Many of these people did not have to work weekends; therefore, they could enjoy being out a little later than usual.

Wyatt Nelson, a Trans-Bridge driver who had a New York City run, was especially glad to be off. He had put in for Christmas Eve to get a four-day weekend, and it was approved. His girlfriend, Grace Saylor, would be joining him here at *Machs Gute* very shortly. She lived in Stroudsburg, about a one-hour drive from Bethlehem, and she was going to stay with him to really enjoy the long weekend. Quite frankly, she was fervently hoping that he would pop the question on Christmas Eve.

The restaurant, famous for its hamburgers, was packed to the gills. SRO but even the customers who weren't seated were happy. The weekend had arrived. For many it would be a four-day weekend, and for some tonight would probably be the beginning of a vacation until the New Year.

When Grace stepped inside, several patrons looked at her with shock etched on their faces. She appeared as though she was a good fourteen months pregnant, and those who saw her could not believe that a woman that far along would be out by herself.

She noticed the stares, and said, "Don't worry, folks. My doctor assured me that this child, a boy by the way, will not be born for another week and a half. It's all good." She smiled and that made the patrons that saw her loosen up a little bit.

Grace worked her way over to Wyatt's table. She was hoping that they would be married before the baby came; but after being together for nearly nineteen years, since they met in ninth grade, one thing or another always delayed the inevitable. Grace would not wait another year. If she wasn't married before the baby was born, it would not be very long afterwards.

They enjoyed each other's company, chowing down on burgers and fries, and as Wyatt drank a few IPAs, Grace had Diet Coke.

She noticed him checking out his watch, wondering what was going on. Wyatt was not good at keeping secrets, so she didn't think he was planning something special. She shrugged it off, but about a half an hour later he said, "How about we get going, honey. It was a long week, and I'd like to spend some alone time with you before we call it a night."

"Ok, that sounds good. Junior is acting up, and I am having quite a bit of discomfort. It will be good to get out of my clothes and throw on a nightgown. Let's go."

She got up and he helped her with her coat. It wasn't super cold outside, so she had decided to wear a lightweight winter jacket. He slipped into his leather Dallas Cowboys jacket, and they worked their way to the front door.

Her eyes lit up when she stepped outside, and a horse drawn carriage was waiting for them.

The driver helped her up into the carriage with Wyatt close behind.

"Honey, taking us on a carriage ride is so sweet of you. I've never been on one."

"This is only the first part of tonight's journey."

They rode down Linden to Broad and then traversed Broad Street until they turned left onto Main Street. The white lights in the trees were spectacular, and after the carriage turned onto Main, they took in the spectacular view of the Star of Bethlehem on South Mountain It appeared to hover in the sky. The famous Bethlehem streetlights radiated a nice, soft glow.

The driver pulled up in front of the hotel and helped them down from the carriage.

Grace thought that they were going to have another drink. When she stepped inside, she stopped dead in her tracks, crying, smiling and laughing all at the same time. Milling around were her parents, her two sisters and one brother, with their families. Wyatt's folks were there as well along with his brother, an Iraq war veteran in a dark blue suit, proudly displaying his Medal of Honor around his neck.

She hugged everyone and then Wyatt got down on one knee in front of her, holding a tiny black box.

He looked up into her eyes and said, "Grace, we've known each other for over nineteen years, neither of us ever wanting to date anyone else. Over the years life got in the way of us getting married. In less than two weeks we are going to have a son. Remember we were struggling to find the perfect name for our perfect boy and your dad suggested we name him Gus. I imagine he will eventually carry that name as a nickname, but your mom was going to hit him with a frying pan. Through all that one thing has always been missing, sharing our lives as man and wife. Hopefully tonight that comes to an end." He opened the box, revealing a beautiful engagement ring. "Grace Saylor, in the presence of our families, I am asking you if you will do me the great honor of being my wife."

When she said yes, he slipped the ring on her finger, stood up and kissed her. Years later she would tell her son that he had never kissed her as passionately as he did when they became engaged.

Both of them had had blood tests recently, and Wyatt had procured the marriage licenses, which they signed five minutes before the wedding ceremony.

He stood up and a female Presbyterian pastor came before them and performed the ceremony. Afterwards, they had a couple of drinks, and some cake, finally retiring to their room, which featured a great view of one of the Top Ten Main Streets in the United States.

The couple sat on the bed, and Grace turned to her husband. "Wow, when you do something, you sure do it right. You have made me the happiest woman on the planet tonight. Even going so far to make sure our cars are here in the parking deck, and our luggage was in the room when we stepped into it. Wyatt, I don't know if any day will ever be as special as this one."

"Grace, I have been crazy in love with you for a long time, and I decided to do this my way because this city is so romantic. I see a lot of very cool places in New York City, and I promise you that we will spend some marvelous weekends there as we go through life. But now I think we should catch some shuteye so we are fresh for the couple of things I have planned for tomorrow."

They got ready for bed; and when they slipped under the covers, feeling the comfort of the magnificent mattress and pillows, they both drifted off to sleep in no time.

December 22nd, 2018

1

Silently closing the back door, Julian stepped outside, trailing Riley on his leash. Julian unzipped his jacket because the air temperature was near sixty degrees. As soon as his paws hit the grass, Riley's leg came up and he relieved himself. He shook and then sniffed where he just peed. They walked around the side of the house to the front sidewalk, where they met Brian Kethledge's neighbor who was obviously a mailman because he was in uniform.

"Hi. I'm Brian Miller. Nice to meet you, Mr. Ross, and who is your four-legged friend?" He squatted down to pet the dog, and then he noticed the prosthetic leg. "What happened to him?"

"Please call me Julian. I'm not old enough to be called Mister." He suppressed a laugh. "Riley lost his leg in a boating accident a few years back when he and his master, the late Graeme McDougal were fishing on Martha's Vineyard. I became Ri's custodian after my friend passed away. He had also lacked a leg, losing it when he was a young man."

Brian continued to pet Riley and he pulled a dog treat from his coat pocket. He stood up and said, "I noticed you coming from Brian's house. Are you staying through New Year's Day?"

"Yes. Petra, my wife, and I came for Sandy's service, arriving on Friday morning around 1:30 AM. Apparently we witnessed a 'miracle' seeing the Star of Bethlehem lit at that time."

Brian laughed. "Two hackers were having a contest to see who could turn on the Star after hours. Personally, I think it should be lit from sunset to sunrise. I love that Star." He choked those words back slightly. "Sorry, but eight years ago I almost lost my wife to a vampire up at that Star. I assume you know pretty much of the story?"

"I do. I read about it at the time. Hard to believe that there was an immortal creature running around in this day and age. I would have only thought them myths, and then five years later when the werewolves were found and destroyed, that blew my mind as well. Last year finding out that angels were real was the icing on the cake. What will come next?"

"Hopefully nothing. Listen, I must get going. Jessie and I have invited a bunch of people to join us for a buffet dinner on Christmas. Brian is invited, so I hope you, Petra, and Riley can join us."

"That would be great. I think he will need a lot of support to help him through Sandy's death. He is almost like a father to me. Doc and my dad served together in Vietnam, and I have known him since I was born. When my dad passed from the effects of Agent Orange, Brian called me every day; and since the advent of the iPhone, we use facetime at least once a week. Okay, I don't want to hold you up any longer. Neither sleet, nor snow, nor rain, etcetera. Have a great day, Brian."

"Yeah, thanks. I have a feeling I will be putting in twelve hours today. There will probably be a few 'sick' calls, and on Monday there will be more, giving some carriers the opportunity to finally get a three-day weekend. At this time of the year we are not allowed to put in for a day off, and those that will take off sick will be hounded unless they bring a doctor's excuse with them when they report back to work. I just can't wait to see the many Christmas cards in red envelopes, handwritten in red ink. So much fun. Okay,

Julian, see you later." He squatted down and petted Riley, pulling another dog treat from his jacket pocket.

2

After a nice long walk, they arrived at the cemetery behind the Central Moravian Church. It only took Julian a couple of minutes to find his parents' graves. He unleashed Riley, knelt, and prayed for them. His immortality had kept him away from his parents for the latter part of their lives, and it hurt him still not to have been there when they passed, four days apart. Had he visited them, he would have been recognized as their son, and he couldn't have that, not having aged.

After saying a lengthy prayer, he stood up and took pictures of the graves with his iPhone, not noticing a man watching him from a distance. Riley was nowhere in sight, but Julian knew the dog would easily find his way back to Doc's house. Since he first met the precocious animal, almost two-hundred and sixty years ago, he had had to rescue him from the puppy police several dozen times. Riley's collar carried Julian's cell number.

The man approached him. "I saw your dog run toward Main Street about two minutes ago. I'm Russ Gallagher, vice-president of the *Bethlehem News,* and you?"

Julian introduced himself and to save time told the reporter why he was here.

"Visiting long-dead relatives is becoming a lost art, I think. I come here often to watch the visitors, to see if I can rustle up any kind of a story, especially at a cemetery this old. Have you a story you want to share with me, Julian?

Julian smiled. He thought he was going to really like this man. "Yes, actually I do. Could we go find a cup of coffee somewhere, and perhaps find Riley as well. Then I'll tell you my story.

"Sure, we'll head to *Billy's Downtown Diner,* and I'll spring for one of the best breakfasts you will ever eat."

3

After Riley gave up chasing the squirrel he saw at the cemetery, he looked around and did not see Julian. He knew he was going to be in big trouble until he found his way back to the nice, warm house they were staying at. Although he usually slept between Julian and Petra, snuggling against Julian's back, he really enjoyed lying on the round rug in front of the fireplace last night. He was so warm, cozy, and safe that he had no intention of moving until he would awaken, or Julian would waken him.

He remembered the time when his master, Graeme, was facing death and told him to find Julian. Riley knew he was smart, but he had no idea where to go. Occasionally he would pick up an old scent and just head off in what he believed was the right direction. Three years ago, on his journey to find Julian, he became totally lost.

4

He walked for a long time, and in the darkness, he didn't see the deep depression, falling into it, impaling himself on a tree limb. He couldn't get loose, and a little while later he 'died'.

Riley reawakened, but he didn't know how he'd be able to work himself from the sharp thin branch that impaled him. He tried to shift his weight both forward and backward, but the impalement occurred at just about his center of gravity. He looked downward and tried to stretch his two good legs downward hoping to be able to get purchase on the ground. He reached out with his front leg as far as he could, feeling his weight shift just slightly, but not enough to touch terrafirma. He was not concerned with time although he was a little hungry and could use some extra energy right now.

He continued struggling, feeling the branch shift a bit, but still not enough to gain a foothold. Riley was one dog that didn't get too frustrated, especially with everything he and Graeme had gone through in over two hundred years. He smiled, realizing that he was over fourteen hundred in dog years.

As he continued with his struggle, he heard a noise and picked up a scent he was not familiar with. He turned his head, searching for the animal making the noise, and soon he saw what it was, and he became more frightened than he'd been in a long time.

It was a wolf, and he looked hungry, but Riley also smelled fear in the predator that was not much larger than him. Riley kept his eyes trained on the grey animal with long, sharp teeth as it circled him trying to figure out why and how his new enemy could not be able to move toward him.

The wolf could smell pain, and he caught a scent unlike any he had ever smelled. The wolf lifted his head and slowly moved closer to Riley, yet not posing too much of a threat. As the wolf closed in, Riley decided to try something that worked with humans. He opened his mouth really wide and whined as though he was looking for a treat. It was enough to stop the wolf and perhaps confuse him into thinking that the impaled dog would not offer any threat. He was hungry, but there was something about the other animal's scent that made him hesitate.

Riley tried every sound and minor movement of friendliness that he could muster, and over the course of perhaps fifteen minutes he managed to signal to the wolf that he needed help.

The wolf had assumed a prone position, still not knowing if he had found a new friend or if the little brown and white animal was a threat. The wolf did notice that the dog only had three legs and one of the three seemed to be broken. He figured that if he did not help him, the animal would probably die and be ravaged by other wildlife. He knew fear from humans and some animals, but he still had to proceed with caution.

He laid there evaluating the dog's position, finally seeing that he was impaled through and through on the branch and that there was probably no way he was going to be able to free himself. The wolf gathered all his knowledge and concluded that if he walked away about fifteen feet and then ran full speed, he could break the branch and free the dog.

Riley watched the wolf walk away and had no idea what was going to happen to him now, but he was hoping that the wolf was not regrouping and planning to attack him. When he saw the wolf turn around and begin to charge him, he tensed and bared his fangs.

The wolf leaped into the air and hit Riley in the side. His full weight, bearing down at great speed, was enough to dislodge the branch from the stump it was attached to and both wolf and dog tumbled for a short distance, winding up entwined around each other.

The wolf got back on his feet and watched Riley get up as well. Riley came over to the predator and licked him. Now that there was trust established, the wolf needed to help his friend get out of this deep ditch and give him a chance to get back to where he lived.

The wolf guided Riley out of the ditch and helped him up the hill to level land. Once they reached the top the wolf nudged Riley with his snout as though telling him he had to go it alone from here. Riley looked at his new friend, wishing he could come with him to take the edge from the loneliness he felt without Graeme and Julian. He loved all the members of the Family, but Graeme and Julian were his two favorites for obvious reasons. He truly wondered if he would ever see Julian again. Graeme had been killed, leaving Riley alone for the first time in his life. He had a daunting task ahead of him, so he hobbled to the road, just keeping far enough away so that he wouldn't get hit. He walked for some time and then he really started to get hungry when he smelled food. He didn't know if he'd be able to get any, but he'd certainly give it his best shot. As a beggar he was right up there with the best of them. He looked back and saw the wolf watching him; and when Riley barked a couple of times, the wolf turned and headed back toward the ditch.

5

As they drove along, listening to an oldies station, Petra was watching the scenery and the road signs. She saw a sign for Gateway Tavern just a couple of miles up the road in Wareham. "Julian, I'm getting really hungry, and that looks like it could be a cool place to wind down a little."

"Sure," he said, "sounds great to me."

If Petra had looked to her right at that moment, she would have seen Riley, but she missed seeing him by a few seconds.

Fifteen minutes later they pulled into the parking lot. The place seemed quite busy, but the food smelled really great from the outside.

There was outdoor seating available, so they decided to sit on the deck and enjoy the view. They were enjoying a beer and some conversation when they heard a diner say, "OMG, look out there, honey. There's a three-legged dog who appears hurt, and he's covered in mud. I wonder where his owner is."

Julian and Petra immediately stood up and saw Riley looking like he had been beaten to crap. He was covered in dried blood, and they saw what appeared to be a tree branch sticking out from the middle of his back and it also looked like a little bit was coming out of the bottom too. Julian whispered to Petra, "We have to get to him first before anyone sees that tree branch and wonders how he could still be alive." He quickly yelled, "Riley, lie down". The dog immediately responded.

Petra said to the people on the deck looking toward Riley, "That's our dog. He wandered off a couple of hours ago, and we'd been looking for him until we got hungry. It seems like he found us."

Julian rushed to him, kneeling and petting him, breaking the top of the branch off while hiding the fact from the people on the deck. When Petra arrived, he said, "Get a blanket from the truck and we'll cover him up. Oh, shit! I didn't leave any money for the drinks. Would you take care of it, please?"

"Sure," she said.

"I'm gonna put Riley in the truck and then I think we better get out of here in a hurry." As she walked away, Julian whispered to Riley, "Everything is going to be okay, old boy. We'll get you fixed up soon, and then we're going on a long trip. I sure wish you could talk and tell me how you got away. It would probably be an incredible story."

Petra came back from the restaurant and hopped in the truck, loving Riley to death as they pulled out of the parking lot and got on the road again.

6

Riley could smell coffee brewing, eggs, bacon and ham being cooked, toast and muffins browning in toaster ovens, and one of his favorites, pancakes on the grill. He was standing behind *Billy's*, and when an employee opened the door, the smells became even stronger. Since Riley became an immortal, it seemed like he was hungry all the time; and now, that he had 'lost' Julian and was starving, he was what humans were calling that emotion, 'hangry'.

He cocked his head and whined, causing the employee, a waitress, to smile. "Hang in there, boy. I'll get you something to eat and drink." She stepped inside and returned a few minutes later with some scraps. Riley licked her hand and did his little dance, causing the young lady, whose nametag read Adrian, to laugh.

She stepped inside and strolled to the table where Julian and Russ were seated. "Sorry for the delay, gentlemen, but I just had to do a good dead for a stray dog out back."

Julian looked up from the menu. "Is he a little brown and white dog with a prosthetic leg?"

"Yes, he does have a fake leg, and he is just adorable."

"He belongs to me. Could I go out the back door and hook him somewhere until I finish breakfast?"

"You sure can."

They strolled out the back door and were greeted with the sight of Riley licking a man's hand, as the man offered him some treats.

The man looked at the waitress and the apparent owner of the dog. "Hi, my name is Billy and I own this restaurant. I see by his tag that this cute dog's name is Riley. Sorry about his leg."

Julian shook his hand. "Thanks, Billy. I'm Julian. Riley has a penchant for getting into trouble. He ran away from me, and I figured someone would call me, or I'd be picking him up at the pound, paying a stiff fine as well."

"Oh, don't be too hard on him. I sense that his life has been pretty good so far, but I think there were a couple of hard knocks on the way."

Julian squatted down and petted his boy. "Ri, you are one lucky puppy, and your punishment will be very minimal, if any at all, because you have probably already forgotten the bad thing you did. Give Billy and Adrian another snookie, so we can go back inside and do what we have to do."

Understanding 'snookie', Riley gave each of them kiss licks on their cheeks, causing everyone to laugh.

7

Petra and Doc were on a mission. There was not enough food for three people and a dog in the house, so a shopping trip to *Wegman's* was second priority. Doc decided to take Petra to breakfast first at *Rudy's,* one of his and Sandy's favorite places. They stopped in almost every Sunday after church, and Brian knew that there would be several patrons offering condolences to him and, of course, asking him who the beautiful young woman was who was dining with him. Some of the old bucks would stare her up and down, trying to remember what it was like escorting a young woman on a date. He had to smile and laugh inwardly. Heck, he was sort of one of those old bucks, too.

Minutes after they were seated, from the corner of his eye, Doc saw his friend, seventy-three-year-old Wayne Muller rise from his seat. As he made his way to their table, the retired gynecologist was a hairsbreadth short of ogling Petra with a twinkle in his eye.

He arrived at the table, with Doc rising and hugging his dear friend. "Petra, this is an old friend of mine, Wayne Muller. He's a retired gynecologist so keep your knees together at all times, or the pervert might want to check you out." The two men laughed, but Petra felt slightly uncomfortable, not understanding older men's humor.

Wayne slightly bowed and said, "It is very nice to meet you, young lady." His eyes twinkled like those of a much younger man.

"And you as well, Doctor Muller." She shook hands with him.

"I've not been a practicing physician for nearly three years, so Wayne is fine."

"You seem a bit young to have retired from a profession, Wayne?" She questioned.

"Yes, I was hoping to practice for many more years, but several years ago I was diagnosed with Parkinson's and that ended my career early. The thing that really bugs me about the disease is that now I can't putt worth a lick, allowing Doc and many other friends to get their hands deep into my pockets. Are you related to this old fart, Petra? By the way, that is a very unusual name. I don't recall ever hearing it before."

"No, my husband and I are friends of him and Sandy and we came in for her funeral service..."

Wayne's pallor turned almost white. "Sandy passed! When did that happen?"

In shock that he forgot to notify his friend, Doc said, "A couple of days ago, we were in an accident. We got T-boned by a truck on her side and there was no way to save her. She's at peace now, my friend. The obituary will be in local papers today. We're having a private service and then I will take her ashes home with me."

"Doc, I'm so sorry. I will let the men in our Bible study know and we will pray for you."

"Thanks, old friend. Now if you don't mind, Petra and I are getting hungry." He sat down, and Wayne walked back to his table. No further words were necessary.

8

At two o'clock the Main Street Bridge was closed off for the hula hoop contest. Every media outlet in the Lehigh Valley was represented, and the event was being filmed from a hovering helicopter, high enough that it's spinning blades would not affect the contest with man-made wind. Al and Lon, along with a handful of helpers, were positioning the contestants, giving them enough space to spin their hoops. Two hundred and ninety-three people of all ages, sizes and sexes were getting in their final practice spins. Using a police megaphone, Al shouted out, "Merry Christmas, everyone, and welcome to the *Retro* hula hoop contest. I am Al Seager, and this is my brother, Lon. Some of you may not have heard all the announcements regarding this contest, so here we go. You are going to be spinning your hoops. If you touch it once it is spinning, or it falls to the street, you will be eliminated. Please be honest with not only us, but yourselves as well. Santa and God could be watching you. If there are any competitors still spinning their hula hoops one-half hour after the contest begins, we will get them together and have a 'hoop-off' to determine the winner. The contest will only last for one-half hour.

"The eventual winner will be awarded a $500 shopping spree at *Retro*. Good luck, everyone. As soon as I blow the whistle, you must begin. The second whistle will announce that the contest has come to an end if it has not ended already. Ok, let's count down from three. Three, two, one." He blew the whistle, and the hula hoops began spinning.

Within the first minute sixty-two contestants were finished, most of them not being able to keep the hoop up, but a few admitted that they would have had to put hands on the hula hoop to continue.

Also filling up the bridge were about a thousand spectators: family members, friends, visitors to the city and seven cops, yelling encouraging remarks to the contestants as the reporters took still pictures, videos, and audio sound bites of the contest. More participants packed it in, staying to cheer on the remainder of the hoopers.

At the halfway mark the total of contestants left dwindled to less than thirty. With nine minutes left there were now only four competitors spinning their hula hoops. At this point, a local TV reporter, Avery Morgan, began interviewing them as the continued to spin their hula hoops.

"My name is Angela Rodriguez. I am seventeen years old, a senior at Liberty High School, and I've been a hula hoop fanatic since I got one for Christmas ten years ago. I'm absolutely certain that I can go for a half an hour because I have done it a couple of times before. This is a great contest, and I can't wait to begin my $500 shopping spree."

"I'm Daniel Gere, a forty-seven-year-old bartender working at *The Bethlehem Brew Works*. I'm a novice hula hooper, having only bought one yesterday. I work out a lot at the gym, and I can jump rope for a long period of time, so I figured I'd have a shot at winning this. If I win, I'm giving my shopping spree to my nephew, Linde. He could use the stuff more than I could."

"Merry Christmas, everyone. My name is Hyram Lasky, and I am the owner of *Lasky's Health*. I played with the hula hoop a lot when I was a kid, and I entered the contest to mainly see if I still had the stamina to control the hoop for this length of time."

"Folks, if you don't know Mr. Lasky, you have probably been living under a rock for the past eight years, but I'll give you a short bio," Avery said. "Hyram Lasky is a retired Bethlehem police detective. In 2010 he and a small band of heroes were able to find and kill the vampire that threatened this city for about a month. Five years later he was also involved in eradicating a large number of werewolves, cloned in a facility deep inside South Mountain. After that incident, he retired. At his retirement party several explosive devices detonated, tearing off both legs and his right arm. Several months later he was confronted by two werewolf clones, turned human, in Wilmington, North Carolina. The female clone had recently given birth to fifteen werewolves, which had to be destroyed. Again, with a small band of heroes, he dispatched them along with three evil witches and a large contingent of earthbound spirits."

"Thanks, everyone," Hy said after a thunderous round of applause from all on the bridge, including the other three competitors still spinning their hoops. He saw that Daniel's hoop was beginning to slide down his waist, and he would probably be out before the thirty-minute mark.

"Finally, folks, I'd like to introduce our final contestant. He is also one of the heroic people who helped rid this city of paranormal creatures. Ladies, gentlemen and kids, I give you Chief Mike McGinnis of the Bethlehem Police Department. Chief, what will you do with the prize if you win?"

"I'm going to purchase toys and games and donate them to my church to give to underprivileged kids."

A minute later, Dan's hoop fell to the street, and he was out. Angela, Hyram, and Mike continued until the whistle sounded, ending the competition. The two men and the young woman congratulated each other, and after consulting with Al and Lon, a winner was determined.

9

After the event, Daniel, Hyram and Mike strolled up Main Street, being applauded almost all the way, and stepped through the front door of *The Brew Works*. The trio needed beer and some food after burning off hundreds of calories participating in the contest.

When their beers arrived, Dan said, "I toast you two men for hanging in till the very end, and for your generosity to Angela, crowing her the champ and giving her the grand prize. I am truly impressed." He lifted his glass to them, and they returned the salute, all three men clinking their glasses together.

Hyram said, "During the contest, I was thinking about her, trying to remember something that was very important. Then it came to me. Angela's mother has shopped at my store many times, but she is a quiet person, and our conversations were usually limited to small talk about the weather, and mundane subjects. One day a couple of months ago she was here with her neighbor and I heard the neighbor ask how her son Jose was feeling. About a week or so later I found out that Jose was paralyzed from the waist down, and he would never walk again.

"I guess my own life was too hectic at that time, and I really didn't give him much thought until today. I talked to Mike and we agreed that he could have a better Christmas if Angela won the shopping spree. Al and Lon had no problem with our decision, and Angela felt she was blessed when she was awarded the shopping spree.

"It is sad that nothing can be done for Jose, but this is the season of miracles, perhaps God has plans for the boy."

December 23rd, 2018

1

Under sunny skies and a crisp forty-degree temperature, the trio of immortals arrived at Becahi, Bethlehem Catholic High School, for the 9 AM traditional worship service of Grace Church. Before the end of January this year, Grace Church was known as First Presbyterian Church of Bethlehem, ECO, and until December of last year, they worshiped at a beautiful old church on Center Street, only a couple of blocks from where the high school stood.

The church members, over twenty-six hundred strong, cast their votes in the spring of 2016 to decide if they would remain with the PCUSA-Presbyterian Church of the U.S.A, or seek membership in FPC-ECO, which stands for A Covenant Order of Evangelical Presbyterian Church. Nearly 80% of the congregation went with ECO, but because of a law that had been in the church's Book of Order, the property and assets were awarded to PCUSA leaving ECO the task of finding a suitable place to worship. They walked down the aisle searching for seats and were noticed by Russ Gallagher. His wife, Joanne, was chatting with the person next to her, giving Russ an opportunity to study Julian Ross again. When he took a video of the young man at the cemetery yesterday, he noticed that Julian was talking to the gravestone. After watching it several times, he was convinced that he was calling the deceased person 'dad'. However, the decedent was buried in the late 1700s. When Russ came home, he Googled Julian Ross and knew he wouldn't get anywhere with nearly 95,000 entries. He was planning on going to the church tomorrow to see what he could find out from their records.

The parishioners enjoyed some wonderful Christmas music as the service progressed. The Word was read by Rev. Dr. Marnie Crumpler, senior pastor, announcements made by Dr. Rev. Manuela Kauer, and then it was time for the sermon to be given by Dr. Rev. Mark Crumpler, Marnie's husband.

2

Julian sat up tall in his comfortable auditorium seat, listening to Pastor Crumpler. He enjoyed the man's soft voice and his demeanor. Over his long lifetime the immortal had heard many preachers, but Crumpler appealed to him immediately.

The pastor loved interjecting local flavor in his sermon, truly noticeable when he told the congregation he wanted to take a poll.

"How many of you are actually traveling for Christmas? You're packing, you're actually traveling, going somewhere. Anybody traveling?" Many hands were raised. "Okay, that's pretty good, but I know that the older you get, the definition of traveling might not mean what it once did. Yeah, we're heading to Catasauqua to see the family."

The laughter began to grow, including from Julian.

In a soft tone, Julian asked, "Brian, is this Catasauqua the pastor mentioned a long distance away?"

Brian giggled. "No, Julian, it's perhaps five miles from Bethlehem."

Julian subsequently laughed again, totally understanding.

Pastor Mark then talked about the traveling he, Marnie, and the kids had done over the years, before he turned serious. "Mary and Joseph had to travel from Nazareth to Bethlehem, a distance of about ninety very hard miles. It probably took them five days. Next week we're going to talk about the Magi, the wise men who traveled for a very long time to leave their gifts for the baby Jesus. And after Jesus was born, he had to travel with Mary and Joseph to Egypt, another very long trip.

Julian's mind went back to the time when he was a youth. His aunt and uncle lived in western Virginia, and they had to go to Williamsburg because Uncle Jedidiah had fallen ill and was not expected to live out the month. He recalled that the journey was arduous, and the trip probably took two weeks. Fortunately, he and his parents were able to spend nine days with Jed before he died. Julian looked down at his left hand. He still wore the ring that his uncle gave him on his deathbed.

"One of my favorite traveling stories was when Buddy had to travel from the North Pole all the way to New York City in search of his dad," Pastor Crumpler said.

Brian leaned over to Julian, during the laugher from the congregation. "That was from a movie. Buddy was one of Santa's elves."

"Of course, you won't find that story in the scriptures," Mark added to more laughter.

"Now, I want you to take a trip, a journey. For what we are doing you won't have to leave your seat. You won't have to leave your home, but this is probably the most significant journey you could make at this time of the year. This journey was first taken by a group of shepherds who were working the night shift. It was a quick commute from the fields outside of Bethlehem to the village where they would search for the Christ child. All you have to do is read Luke Chapter Two beginning at verse eight."

The immortals listened intently because as time passed, they would take many journeys, but would any be as poignant as the one the shepherds took?

"The shepherds told everyone they saw about the story of Christ's birth. Even if you only come to church once a year, which is usually at this time, you learned this story. If you never even attend church, you probably learned the story from *A Charlie Brown Christmas* when Linus takes center stage and recites Luke 2. But Linus stops the story too soon. He stops before the shepherds look at each other and say, 'Let's go see.' I want you all to take this journey. What will you do to share this good news? If you really heard the story, it needs a response. Who is the good news of great joy for?"

The congregation responded with the word 'everyone'.

"Yes. Jesus came to us as a savior. He did not come as a teacher or a prophet. We need him as a savior. Things will not be made right by a teacher or a coach but only by a savior.

"I came across a painting of Mary, Joseph and Jesus in the stable. Nobody was there, and Mary looked exhausted while Joseph looked overwhelmed. If you are a parent, you will probably understand this. The world is not perfect. Jesus came into a broken world where he could mend us and make us whole.

"What will we do with what we just heard? Some people have lost their faith, and we must look deeper to be able to share this good news. Walk out of here with three words. 'Let's go see.' Look into your faith. We gather, and then we scatter all over the valley.

"The shepherds returned to the fields, to the same job, the same grass, the same sheep. We are here to tell the story. Thanks be to God."

3

After the service, the trio drove to *Rudy's* where they had a great meal and shared fellowship with some of the congregation members.

Julian had never given much thought to the passing years of his immortality because, unless someone removed his head, he would be here as long a time itself. Was it his duty to spread the good news as he saved a small number of people from the sting of death? He had a great 'family' until they were taken from him by one of their own. He knew he had a lot to think about, and during his time here in Bethlehem, he hoped to speak to the Crumplers about his life and what meaning it should have to Christianity.

On the way home Petra said, "Honey, I have never asked you this, and I don't know why I need to know this now, but which was the hardest of your 'deaths' to forget? Hell, I don't even know how many times you 'died.'"

"Those questions actually *are* easy to answer, Petra. I have died seven times since first becoming immortal. I have not ever been as scared as I was when I died at the Alamo.

"I'd been traveling around with Davy Crockett and his small band of hunter/fighters. Because he always impressed me as ten-feet tall and bulletproof, Crockett seemed to always need to mix it up with someone, somewhere, and when he heard about Texas' fight for independence, he knew he had to help them out. He gave his men the choice of coming to Texas with him or going back home to their families. Nine chose to go back home. Davy had the rest of us write letters to our families in case we never made it back. He was a tough cookie and I thought that anything he'd get into; he'd fight his way out.

"Six of us arrived at the Alamo on February 8th, meeting William Travis and Jim Bowie not long after we arrived. Those two men did not get along, giving Davy an opportunity to use skills he learned in Congress to get the two leaders to tolerate one another. I listened in to some of the conversation he was having with Travis and Bowie, and I was amazed with the legendary man's power of persuasion. They then began preparations to defend the Alamo, which was an old church and not too sturdily built to survive artillery for a long period of time.

"On February 23rd, a large contingent of Mexican troops arrived and set up camp. They flew the red flag of 'No Quarter', sealing the Alamo's doom. There were only 156 effective fighters manning the old church. Fourteen more were hospitalized. It wasn't rocket science to know that if Santa Anna wanted the Alamo, we were all goners.

"I got hit a couple of times, and fortunately only Crockett saw that I had been wounded. I had told Davy about my immortality as soon as we decided to stay at the Alamo. I told him that if he were to die, and I was nearby, I would give him the gift. My luck held out pretty well until March 5th. I was helping out carrying wounded men into the chapel when a cannonade began. A ball exploded next to me, and shrapnel filled my belly and my chest. The wounded man I had been carrying died when he got hit in the head.

"I remember dropping like a stone, but I saw an overturned wagon that would be my 'home' for the night and the next day. Some of the men saw me get hit, and figured I would be dead soon, so they left me to myself. When I reawakened under the wagon, at daybreak on the 6th, the Mexicans had fought their way into the compound, killing everyone in sight except for any women they saw. I must have moved, because I was bayonetted in the side. It wasn't fatal, allowing me to witness the remainder of the slaughter.

"All the dead bodies, including myself, though still alive, were taken outside and buried in a mass grave. I worked my way out, and by midnight I was able to grab a horse and leave the area."

Petra placed her hand on Julian's and kissed him lightly on the cheek. Julian was crying.

After several long moments, he recovered. "Sorry, folks. Recalling what happened at the Alamo always affects me. I don't think I ever spoke at that length about the battle, and I hope I didn't make you both too uncomfortable."

"Julian, in 'Nam, you and I had gone through many things during our bouts of combat that people who haven't walked the walk could even begin to imagine. The courage you and the other defenders possessed was more than admirable. I know there were a few times when I thought we were going to be overrun, giving our lives to protect the piece of ground beneath our feet, and I don't think there is anything scarier. To suffer night and day cannonade for two weeks is something I can't even picture. Thank you for giving your life-that time-to help give Texas a chance to be free." He hugged Julian for a very long time, both shedding tears.

"Thanks, Doc. There have been a lot of incidents in my very long life but nothing like that before or since."

"Julian, I do have one question. Did Crockett die a hero or not?"

"I honestly don't know. He was still fighting before I was killed because I saw him directing men as to where they should fire, and at one time, he actually fired up a cannon at the enemy. I know over the years, in movies and books, he has been portrayed as a hero. When played by Fess Parker in the *Disney Davy Crockett* series, he is seen using his rifle as a club, taking out Mexicans as they followed him up stone steps to the top of the structure. In John Wayne's *The Alamo,* Davy is killed in the final defense when he is run through with a lance just as he ignites the powder magazine. When Billy Bob Thornton portrayed him, Davy was executed by many Mexican bayonets.

"I just don't know how he was killed, but I don't think he died a coward. I believe he went down swinging. Sorry I can't give you a definitive answer to your question."

4

When they arrived back at Brian's house, Riley was happy to see them, giving sloppy, wet, dog kisses to the trio.

Julian hooked him up to the leash and out the door they went. Petra needed a few minutes, but she wanted to go for a walk on Main Street and perhaps do a bit of shopping. She wanted to get a nice gift for Doc, and she also felt she should get gifts for Brian and Jessie Miller, since they were going to offer their hospitality on Christmas.

They first walked to Walnut Street in order to come onto Main Street by the Central Moravian Church. Before arriving at the Moravian Book Shop, they saw several little huts where vendors were selling their products and crafts.

"Doc, those huts are really cute. Are there any more?" Petra inquired.

"Yes, once we go further up the street there is a little courtyard where more huts are set up. The city has been doing this for years and it's great because some of the stuff they sell can't be bought in local stores."

Lots of shoppers were walking both ways on the tiny brick pavements, ducking into stores, looking for that special last-minute gift. Petra saw a store that she wanted to check out. *Seasons Taproom* carried olive oils, vinegars, pastas, and gift sets. The men and Riley waited outside while she tasted some of the products on display. After about ten minutes she settled on a Paella Gift Basket for Brian and Jessie. The set contained a paella pan, cookbook, rice, and extra ingredients to make a great meal with the addition of meat, fish or vegetables.

After strolling through the village huts in the courtyard, Petra wanted to stop at *Donegal Square* to look around in the Irish shop. It didn't take her long to get a smile on her face. Twenty minutes later she exited the store with a Bethlehem Midnight Star, a sweater for herself, and one sweater each for Julian and Doc.

She walked over to *The Bethlehem Brew Works* where the men stopped off for a drink.

5

Petra stepped inside and found Julian and Brian sitting at the bar, guarding an empty seat between them, and she sat down. "Where's Riley?"

Julian told her that he gave a Moravian College student twenty bucks to walk Riley for a half an hour. He said that Riley took to the young woman immediately, and he was certain there wouldn't be any problems. Noticing the large package, Julian asked, "Anything for me?" He seductively rubbed her leg.

"Maybe, but if you don't stop what you're doing, I might not give it to you."

Doc took a sip of his beer and said, "Get a room, you two."

After they finished their drinks, Julian gave the dog walker a call, and she returned with Riley two minutes after the trio stepped outside.

6

Less than a minute later Russ Gallagher caught up with them as they walked down Main Street.

"Hi folks, funny running into you guys today. How are you all doing?"

Julian looked at him and nodded. "Russell, this is my wife, Petra, and my friend Brian Kethledge."

They both nodded at him as well and shook his hand.

"If you folks could spare a half an hour, I'd like to talk with Julian about his visit to his ancestor's grave day before yesterday."

Passivity gave way to activity on their faces, but they all agreed to have a talk with the newspaper man. Doc and Petra didn't know what this was all about, but there was cause for concern if Russ had been digging into Julian's past.

"Sure, Russ. That would be fine. Since we're here at the Hotel Bethlehem, we could go in for a drink and a good talk. I'll see if a valet will take care of Riley for a little while." While the others went inside, Julian strolled to a valet and asked if he'd watch Riley for about a half an hour. He pulled a twenty-dollar bill from his wallet and handed it to the young man.

After joining the others in the lounge, a waitress came to them and took their drink orders.

"On Friday I saw Julian spending a great deal of time viewing a gravestone, and I think he was praying or talking to the decedent because his lips were moving. I took my phone out and shot a video while he was doing this. Also, I was given a good reason to approach him when I saw Riley chase a squirrel without Julian seeing him.

"I went to him and asked if he was remembering a long dead relative. He told me it was his great, great, something grandfather. We chatted for a moment and then he said, "Would you mind walking with me while I look for my dog? Perhaps we could get a cup of coffee."

94

Their drinks came. Julian handed the waitress a fifty-dollar bill and told her to keep the change.

"I studied the video I took, and I am confident that Julian was using the word *'dad'.*"

When the trio began looking around to see if anyone was paying attention to their conversation, Russ softened his voice. "Yesterday I visited Central Moravian and after quite a bit of research, I came up with Jerimiah's name and family members. His wife was Martha and he had a son named Julian." Russ took a pregnant pause waiting for a reaction. To his consternation his three companions did not change the expressions on their faces.

"Because Jerimiah was one of the first to settle in Bethlehem, there were journals that I was allowed to peruse, and I found out that Julian left the country when he was about thirty-two, and I couldn't find out if he ever returned." He stopped talking again.

"The Internet is an amazing tool, folks. You know there are almost ninety-two thousand entries with the names Julian and Ross, four-hundred and seventy-seven thousand for Petra Ross, and twelve thousand more for Brian Kethledge. I didn't believe in a lot of things until I met an angel last year, so I'm going to throw out a theory." Again, he lowered his voice and lowered his head so as not to be captured on a security camera. The others leaned in toward him.

"I think you are the original Julian, and I also think that Brian 'Doc' Kethledge served with *you* in Vietnam, not your father..."

Julian interrupted. "You, my friend, are an amazing newshound, and yes I am the original Julian. I don't want anything more said here because I don't want to be exposed, so would you and your lovely wife please join us tonight for dinner at Doc's house? At that time, I'll tell you anything you want to know. I will also hope that you not share anything with your readership, close friends, or anyone with whom you normally associate."

Russ raised his head and nodded. He reached for Julian's hand.

7

Al and Lon were having the best time and making a huge amount of money at the same time. Among the different items they had sold so far were a Gort robot from the movie, *The Day The Earth Stood Still*, back in 1951. Lon remembered the film well because he had seen it over thirty times since he was a kid. Two customers were interested in it, and Lon suggested they each write an amount on a slip of paper-something the owners would be doing often-and the highest bidder would win. The winning amount was $150, edging the other bidder out by five dollars.

Some of the other items sold were three pairs of Texas Ranger Double Cap Gun Sets including holsters. Four happy people walked out with Switch Blade Hair Combs, popular around nineteen-fifty. One of the customers was bald, so that was really a fun sale. One box contained about 50 Retro Flyer Balsa Wood Airplanes that virtually flew off the shelves-no pun intended.

A popular item for many boys was to walk from the store wearing Civil War Union Blue Kepi Caps, while several girls wanted Cowgirl Pink and Silver Cap Guns and Schylling Piano Horns.

Al was opening boxes in the back room, and he opened several that contained the same item: wood-handle jump ropes. He called his brother back for a moment. "Lon, look at these. I think we could do a jump rope contest in the future. I don't know if Chief McGinnis would close the bridge again, but we could probably hold the contest in a nearby park."

"Brother, I like the way you think," Lon said.

8

Joanne Gallagher sat on the bed, wrapping gifts. She had spent the past year relearning to do many things that she hadn't done in two years, and the feelings of just taking a long run, bicycling around the city, and taking care of Russ and the house again, were exhilarating. Yesterday's visit to her doctor confirmed that every body part was functioning perfectly. She had lost the twenty-five pounds she gained while confined to her wheelchair, and her mental faculties had returned. Being in full control of her body and her mind was the best thing that had happened to her since marrying Russ.

She still had no idea why God had seen fit to send Victoria Christmas to her when she was as close to the bottom of the barrel as she could get. Thankfully her suicide attempts were just that-attempts. Now she truly realized what a gift life was. Over the next unknown amount of years she had left, she decided that she would commit more to the needs of her church and charities, giving as much as she possibly could. She and Russ would never have to worry about any financial problems because of the amount of money they had earned for their stories. There was even a rumor floating around that a local production company wanted to make a film about the paranormal events that had occurred over the past eight years.

However, now she had to get busy with wrapping the gifts and preparing something to take to the Miller's house on Christmas. There was where she would give a gift to someone that would change his life forever.

9

Hyram and Susan Lasky were having a blast at the store. They had purchased a hoagie platter from Wegman's, along with a cheese and cracker plate to munch on for whomever would visit the shop today. There was also a large bowl of punch to drink. They had a roll of tickets, giving one to each customer who wrote his or her name and phone number on the back, to win a one-thousand-dollar shopping spree.

Hyram stood behind the cash register watching Susan work, re-stocking shelves, and straightening up. She was beautiful and he considered himself extremely fortunate to have her as his wife. She always seemed to know what to do to cheer him up when he was down and how to gently bring him back to earth when his ego became larger than his hat.

Susan caught him staring and smiled. She also thought that she was fortunate to have Hy for a life partner. He took care of her physical and mental needs all the time. Both drifted off into space far too often, thinking back to those horrible weeks at the end of 2016 and the beginning of 2017. Losing an arm was never on her things to do list, but there are many things that can happen to a person in a lifetime.

Of course, when they were on that great vacation at Wrightsville Beach, she never thought that she would have to deal with werewolves again. Fighting witches and earthbound spirits were not in her plans either. She prayed every day that she and Hy would never have to deal with any of that again.

10

Riley was curled up in front of the fireplace, dreaming about Scotland and Graeme. They both had loved where they lived on a hillside above the Loch.

Nearly every day was an adventure because, unlike today, there was not much readily available for people and dogs to eat and drink. They had to hunt and fish and boil water to assure that they wouldn't get sick from the bacteria that was always floating around in it. There were springs that provided clean water, but to get to them meant an arduous, all day trip. Graeme would get all the empty water bags from a storage area in the cabin, and he would tie them to the saddle, hop on the horse, and then they would be off.

Riley loved his master with all his heart. He vividly remembered when he selected the one-legged man to be his companion. The dog was in a kennel in Glasgow. He had been born about five weeks before, along with four other dogs, and when he saw Graeme, he knew he wanted the man to take him home.

Graeme had come into the city to hopefully find a dog, and when the little brown and white puppy began barking and jumping up and down, the old Scot smiled and reached over the low fence to pet the happy animal. Riley immediately licked his face, and Graeme was sold. He bartered with the owner until finally settling upon a fair price.

After that day, the pair were inseparable until Graeme was killed. The last three years with Julian and Petra were also mainly wonderful, happy times too. After Riley met Doc, he fell in love with that man, too.

The doorbell rang, and Riley flew to door to see who was coming to visit and if they had treats.

11

Russ and Joanne stepped into the house, bearing gifts of wine, cheese and a rawhide bone for Riley. Russ tossed it across the room and Riley took off, catching it in mid-air, dangerously close to the Christmas tree. He landed on the floor, laid down and began chewing.

The human couple and the immortals laughed for several moments before Brian said, "Welcome to my home, folks. Please give me your coats and I'll hang them up."

Before taking off their coats, Russ handed the wine to Petra and Julian took the cheese tray from Joanne.

They strolled into the living room and sat down.

When Brian joined them, Joanne said, "You have a really beautiful home, Brian."

"Thanks, Joanne. I'll give you the nickel tour in a little while, and since Julian and Petra have come to visit, I'm very comfortable with being called Doc as well as Brian. Several of my local friends, veterans actually, knew I had been a medic in 'Nam, and they call me Doc, too."

Julian filled everyone's wine glass and passed the cheese tray around. He noticed Russ watching him and when he sat down, he said, "Russ, I have a feeling you want to cut to the chase and hear my story before any other conversation will be considered."

"If you all don't mind, yes, I would like to hear that. I guess you could give me the short version and then I could ask questions."

Julian laughed. "It's not too easy to condense two - hundred and seventy-one years, but I'll do my best. Doc, Petra, if I begin to get too long-winded, please throw something at me."

Riley had already finished his bone, so after giving everyone a couple of sniffs and begging several pieces of cheese, he yawned. Circling three times, he plopped on the floor in front of the fireplace.

"You know, believing that there are immortal people is a tough gig, but a three-legged dog as well totally blows me away," Russ stated, reaching down and patting his head.

"Yeah, it is, and I honestly didn't know if my power would save an animal. I am so glad I could and have him walk through eternity with us. Before I continue, I have to tell you folks that an old friend of Doc's, Connie Abernathy will be joining us shortly. She was released from the hospital a couple of hours ago."

Russ smiled. "Is she the woman police officer you were able to save a couple of nights ago?"

"Touché, Russ. I had a feeling you might figure that out." Julian lifted his glass in a toast.

12

Earlier, Connie Abernathy had been released from the hospital when nothing could be found wrong with her. Many of the doctors and nurses could not believe that she could walk away from that accident without as much as a scratch. Every vital sign was a perfect number, all her labs were right on the money as well, and all X-rays were clean.

She took an Uber to her house; and when she walked inside, the magnitude of what had occurred in the past fifty some hours finally hit her like a fastball to the gut. A man named Julian Ross saved her life by giving her his blood. She was now immortal, and the only way she could die would be to have her head severed from her body.

When she was a kid she loved to read and watch stories dealing with immortality. Her favorite book being *This Immortal,* by Roger Zelazny. Her favorite movie was *The Picture of Dorian Gray.* She was also a big fan of the TV show, *Dark Shadows.* Connie was not a kid anymore, but the thought of not having to die was reprehensible. Her daughter was still in her thirties, but anything could cause her death at any time. What would she think about her mother-seeing her stay the same as she grew older? Connie and Debbie would have to have a long talk about this. Her grandson was only eleven. Would Connie be able to tell him that she would never grow old and that all her family would be long dead before anything might happen to her?

She had to think about Brian. He just lost Sandy less than a week ago. How would it look if he began keeping company with her this soon after his wife's death? People would talk, and he would be looked upon as a small person for not giving himself time to grieve.

Connie would be joining her new, immortal family this evening for dinner, and she was sure she would have many questions for them.

13

After she arrived and was introduced to Riley, letting the small dog lick her face for a couple of minutes, she went to the bathroom to wash up.

Dinner was ready, and everything was delicious. Connie thought she had more of an appetite than usual, and it caused her to ask, "Will I gain weight over the years ahead of me?"

Petra answered with a smile. "No, Connie, our bodies will no longer change, and I like that part of immortality. I always had a problem keeping my weight perfect, but after I died, I found I could eat anything and not gain an ounce."

Talk about Christmas filled the dinner hour, each of them sharing some of their favorite Christmas stories and gifts they received.

When it was Julian's turn, dessert and coffee were on the table.

"I've been thinking about this question for some time because Brian and Jessie Miller want us to share our most memorable Christmas story, but I'd like to share it with you all, first.

"I've mainly never been a real political man, but back in 1960 I was truly enamored with Jack Kennedy. I thought the young man, if he were elected president, would lead America to many great opportunities for countless people. These endeavors would create new, exciting businesses and increase the wealth of the country tenfold.

"After becoming a member of the Kennedy election team, I moved in with Graeme that summer in order to be able to get to Hyannis quickly when the young man or his family needed him to be close. I had Kennedy's ear, and I offered him a great many suggestions to help him in the polls.

"When he won, I was ecstatic, and I followed him to Washington to work as a staffer in the White House.

"To make a long story short I was thrilled to help Mrs. Kennedy prepare the White House for Christmas of 1961. That was such an honor. On the final day of decorating, she took me aside and said, 'Julian, you have been a hard worker and a great friend of Jack and I, and we would like you to attend our private family Christmas celebration in the residence.'

"I thanked her and panicked. What was I going to get for the president, the first lady and the first kids for Christmas presents? I called Graeme and asked him for some suggestions. One-month old John-John probably would not be too tough to buy for, but Caroline? Jackie? Jack? 'Son,'" he said, I think I can take care of the president, but I would like to ask you to arrange a meeting with him. I can be in DC in a couple of days with a two-hundred and fifty-year-old bottle of the finest scotch whisky I ever made.'

"Just that moment, the president was passing by my office door. I said, 'Mr. President, can I have a moment of your time, please?' He nodded and walked into my office. 'I am talking to my oldest and dearest friend, and he would like to ask you something.' Kennedy said, 'Sure, hand me the phone.' He listened to Graeme talk for a minute or two and then said, 'It would be a pleasure to have you join us for Christmas.' The president walked from my office without another word. 'Graeme, you have such a knack, you know.' 'Thanks, Julian. I'll see you Christmas Day. Oh, I also have a box of fine Cuban cigars he might like.' He hung up.

"On Christmas morning I was summoned to the residence. Graeme, dressed to the nines in a formal Scottish kilt, was by my side. He was carrying the bottle of Scotch and a box of cigars for the president. I was carrying a doll for Caroline and a simple silver bracelet and necklace for Jackie.

"The family was seated together on a couch. The president stood up and approached us to shake our hands. "Graeme, you look marvelous, and I know we will enjoy your gifts a little later. Julian, thank you so much for all you have done for me to get me to this office. If you turn around, you will see I have a gift for you. I turned and, astonishingly, there stood Paul and Shannon. Riley was held on a leash by Paul, but when Caroline saw him, she raced over to pet him. For the first time in nearly thirty years my Family was together along with the First Family.

"Graeme, did you hypnotize the President of the United States?"

"Perhaps a wee bit, Laddie. Enjoy it."

"After the family celebration concluded, my family was given access to the library where we talked for hours.

"Until I met Petra, that was my best Christmas ever."

They retired to the living room again where Julian spent the better part of two hours telling his life story

December 24th, 2018

1

Russ Gallagher watched his wife sleeping. Last night was amazing, hearing Julian's life story and the stories of how Petra and Doc received the gift, along with Connie. He had thought that human immortals could not exist. Impossible? Perhaps, but so were vampires and werewolves, and he actually met an angel. He looked over at his sleeping wife, healed of her paralysis last Christmas Eve by Victoria Christmas. He would never disbelieve anything again.

Joanne Gallagher had been a strong, young woman, very athletic with the world as her oyster, many marathons to be run waiting for her. The accident had changed her. She tried to remain positive, praying for a miracle, but she felt that God was not listening to her. After a few futile months praying for her physical salvation although she would never lose her faith, she prayed for other people. After she was healed, she told Russ about her futile attempts to even kill herself to relieve him of his duty as her caregiver.

"Honey," he had said, "when we married, we vowed for better or worse, in sickness and health, till death do us part. Had you not been healed I would have loved you as much or even more than the day we said those words."

He got up and went downstairs for his first cup of coffee and to read the *Bethlehem News*. The front page carried a story about the gentlemen who had been portraying St. Nicholas at Christmasfest Market for the past two years.

2

After a long career in property management Mark Talijan, a senior property manager at the CBRE Group on the 10th floor of Tower 6 in Allentown, took up the mantle of being the co-St. Nick along with Rick Bachl at Bethlehem's Christmasfest Market. About 20 years ago, while at First Valley Bank in Bethlehem, Talijan was tapped to play the part of breakfast Santa at a work function to bring some departments together for the holidays.

"Nobody wanted to do it, so I decided to give it a try to see what the magic was."

Bachl said that after he retired, he pursued an interest in theater. He had been an architect with W2A Design Group. He performed in local shows and did voiceover work in New York City. I become marginally famous after a one-day gig being an extra, in a funeral scene. The film, Getting Grace, was directed by Bethlehem native Daniel Roebuck.

Three years ago, after performing a script reading, he was approached with the idea of taking up St. Nicholas at Christmasfest Market.

"I had thought about it years earlier, while acting in other gigs but I just never pursued the idea. I should have checked it out sooner because doing it is really magical. I love building model toys but listening to the kids share their Christmas lists is very rewarding." He laughed.

Talijan said, "One young boy sat on my lap and said, 'You're not the real Santa.' I thought his folks would have a heart attack. My Santa cap was not the right shape and I do not pack the necessary weight. "You're right," I replied, "but I am the real St. Nicholas."

Bachl stated, "I love this job, because portraying Santa or St. Nick is very important. Children of these ages are very impressionable, so I never take my job lightly."

Their training was wrapped up in what they already had: personality and life experience.

Talijan said, "You either have it or you don't, and you know that right away. Not everyone can portray the big guy."

They all have to do the same things for kids: level with them and open up to them, but you can't give everything away.

"I could write a book," Talijan offered with a belly laugh. "Kids like to ask trick questions, like, 'Where are your reindeer?' "I only bring two because it's such a short flight from the North Pole to Bethlehem. They stay at the Bethlehem police barn with the horses."

Bachl told about the eight-year-old girl who flatly stated, both hands on her hips, 'My Elf on the Shelf must have told you what I want for Christmas, so why don't you tell me.' "I had to think about that one for a moment and explained, "Elves and Santa both have bonds of secrecy, so he never really told me. He tells my worker elves." You gotta be creative in this business.

"Another one asked, 'How old is St. Nick?' "I responded 'I'm not real young, but I'm not real old either.' I could see a young girl thinking about this, and then she said, 'I think you're forty-six.' I nodded and gave her the thumbs up."

They both interjected that once you put the suit on, you are in character. You have to become the right character quickly because kids pick up on it very quickly.

"I was caught out of character once," Talijan stated. "I had the suit on at home and had to get something out of my car. My 30-year-old neighbor standing frozen on the *sidewalk, discovered that his neighbor was Santa, and that my sled was a Chevy Impala."*

3

After a nice, leisurely breakfast with Joanne, who wasn't really hungry but had some dry toast and coffee, Russ Gallagher went to the office. As he stood at the window watching the buildup of final day Christmas shoppers, he saw Julian walking Riley. Some of the bricks in the sidewalk were not lying flat. He saw a squirrel dart from a tree, and Riley began to chase it. Julian must have had the leash very loose in his hand, and probably re-gripped it when he felt the dog pull. Three stumbles later he fell to the sidewalk, but a passerby helped him up.

Russ hurried across the street and saw a bone sticking out from Julian's arm. A couple of moments later, the fracture healed itself.

"It was pretty interesting seeing how quickly you heal. Are you in a hurry or would you and Riley like to come over to my office for a cup of coffee? I think I might have something Riley would like, too."

"Sure, that would be great."

After pouring coffee for them both, Russ brought the steaming cups to his desk and set them down. He took a seat in his comfortable leather chair and gave Riley a chew toy that he found in a desk drawer.

"You didn't tell us much about Riley last night. I assume he is immortal as well? Would you like to tell me about him now.?"

"Certainly. Ten years after receiving the gift of immortality I was sent to live with a friend of my father. Graeme McDougal lived on a hill overlooking Loch Ness, along with his two-year-old dog Riley. Graeme was suffering with a disease that was actually a cancer, but my immortal blood was able to cure him.

"Eight years later, Graeme and Riley were in his boat on the Loch, fishing, when a fast-moving storm hit. The boat crashed into the rocks, and a shard of wood took off Riley's leg. Graeme managed to save his pet, but his heavy clothing was taking them under. By the time I arrived both were breathing their last. I cut the palm of my hand, forcing them both to drink some of my blood, and they came back to life a little while later."

"I am totally blown away by all of this, and not just you and the other immortals but everything that has happened in this city over the years. I wonder if the town is cursed to be visited by both good and bad paranormal creatures. The vampire and the werewolves were the bad, and Victoria Christmas and you are the good. I must wonder what will come next. So, where are you and Riley off to?"

"We're just out for our morning constitutional. I love walking around this city. If I don't see you later or tomorrow, I'll see you tomorrow night at the Millers. Have a good day, Russ."

"You too."

4

A police car and an ambulance were parked outside of *Retro.* With lights still flashing two officers and two paramedics rushed inside the store as a small crowd began to gather. Seeing the emergency vehicles, Russ Gallagher raced to the scene too.

He pulled his press pass and walked past the one officer who was controlling observers both inside and out. He saw the paramedics and the officer working on a man who was lying face up on the floor. He was obviously in considerable pain, clutching his chest and crying out how bad it hurt.

The victim was Al Seager. He was taken to the hospital where they admitted him for a mild heart attack. He would return to work early in 2019. He and Lon would hold the jump rope competition in the spring in the large field at the Murray H. Goodman campus of Lehigh University.

5

After work Mike McGinnis headed home. He and Sara were planning on spending a quiet Christmas Eve with dinner, Candlelight service at Grace Church, and then opening their gifts to one another. His old partner Nikki Lawson said she might stop by for a drink between six and six-thirty. He hadn't seen her since she resigned from the department shortly after the bombing at Hyram Lasky's retirement party.

She was the one to find her husband dead, one of the 23 victims of the explosion. He knew she had moved away, but he didn't know she returned to Bethlehem until he got a call from her three days ago wanting to get together. Mike hoped that if she did come over for a drink-she had refused a dinner invitation-he and Sara could talk her into going to church with them.

They knew that Nikki had renounced God after Chuck was killed, and it hurt them because she had been a faithful servant for her whole life, but sometimes one life event can change a person in a virtual heartbeat.

6

After arriving at home, he went upstairs and took off his uniform, hanging it neatly on a hook on the back of the closet door. He placed his weapon and holster in a safe inside the closet and locked it. He heard water running in the bathroom, knocked on the door, and then stepped inside. He had to knock because one time he came in just as Sara was stepping out from the shower. She screamed bloody murder because he scared the crap out of her. She hated being taken by surprise and told him in no uncertain terms that 'if you ever scare me again, McGinnis, I will kick your butt so high and so far, that you might never come back down.'

She stepped from the shower and said, "Hi Honey. How was your day?"

"It was good, pretty quiet, and I'm looking forward to dinner, church, and unwrapping gifts. You?"

"Not bad, Chief. Heather Harrison and I had one issue with two cars trying to get the same parking space. One was backing in and the other was pulling in and neither would give up."

"So, what did you do?"

"Neither of us wanted to issue a citation, so we had both the drivers step out and I did an old-fashioned coin flip. It worked, too. The loser got back in her car and just drove away with no arguing or anything."

"Pretty cool there, Sergeant. I'm proud of..."

"Mike, what did you just call me?"

"I called you 'Sergeant'. It won't be official for a couple of days, but you passed the test and you're one of three who are going to be promoted on January 2nd. Congrats, Sara."

"That is great. I've been hoping for this for a long time. I think I will be a terrific sergeant."

"You will be a great sergeant for sure. Now I have another surprise for you. Today I got a call from Nikki Lawson. She's in Bethlehem starting today until January 7th. She said she had something important to tell us, and she asked if she could stop by around six."

"That would be good. I'm making baked chicken, pasta, and veggies for dinner and there will be plenty. You told her we have to leave around seven fifteen to get to candlelight service?"

"I did. Are you ready for this! She wants to come to church with us."

"That is incredible. After she lost Chuck in the explosion, and renounced God, I thought we'd never see her in a church again."

"Yeah, me too. I'm going to grab a quick shower. I'll be down soon to give you a hand getting dinner ready.

"Okay, see you soon." Sara almost floated down the stairs with the great pieces of news she just heard.

7

Nikki Lawson stepped out from the car, glimpsing the Star of Bethlehem over the tops of trees and houses. She had missed Bethlehem a lot; but after losing Chuck, she lost her zest for life and the last thing she wanted to do was pray. God took her husband away, and she would never forgive Him.

She sauntered up to the front door, carrying a bottle of wine, a loaf of bread, and a container of salt, since this would be the first time, she was visiting Sara and Mike's new house. After watching *A Wonderful Life* for the umpteenth time, she recalled the scene where these gifts were presented to a new homeowner. Bread was given to stave off hunger, wine so there would never be thirst, and salt to season their lives. It was probably a little corny, but she was sure Mike and Sara would appreciate the gesture. She rang the bell.

Sara ushered her old friend inside and put the gifts on a small table in the hallway. She then took Nikki's coat and hung it in the closet.

They walked into the living room and sat down to the warmth of a gas fireplace.

Nikki looked around and checked out the Christmas decorations. Sara had made many of them herself, and the house looked absolutely lovely.

Mike shuffled down the stairs; and when he saw Nikki, he smiled and gave her a hug and a kiss on the cheek. "Welcome home, partner. It's great to see you again, and you look wonderful."

"Thanks, Mike. I feel wonderful. I'm bursting to tell you my news, and I'm not going to wait any longer." She held out her left hand. "I'm married."

"Nikki, that's great. How, when, where is he?"

She laughed. "It's one of those impossible to believe stories, and when Larry arrives later tomorrow, we'll tell you guys the whole story. We married six weeks ago, and I have known him since February 4th, 2016, after meeting him under unusual circumstances. I will tell you this, he can't be here tonight because of a job-related commitment."

The two cops knew they wouldn't get anything more out of Nikki, and they didn't even try.

8

As they walked into the auditorium at Becahi, Sara told Nikki what had happened with the church breakup and how ECO wound up here.

Rev. Dr. Marnie Crumpler took the stage to give her Christmas message. Nikki listened intently, nodding when Marnie said, "Had the birth occurred today, it would have been big, being covered by major cable news stations, but on that first Christmas God's glory showed up with a whisper and the cry of a baby. Before this God always showed up big.

"Think about how world leaders make an entrance in today's world. They have security, limos and a lot of fuss. I heard that on Queen Elizabeth's last visit to America she brought so much stuff with her. She brought 4000 pounds of luggage including two outfits for every occasion, a mourning outfit in case someone died, forty pints of plasma, and, get this, two white kid leather toilet seat covers. She brought her hairdresser, two valets and a host of other attendants.

"But God, when he came into the world, He brought nothing. Nothing. Ever since that Christmas night Christmas Eve has been different. When you leave tonight, if you should go into downtown Bethlehem, you would see a reminder of what happened in 1741 when the town of Bethlehem began. Only the word Bethlehem will be lit up on top of the *Hotel Bethlehem*. Back in 1968 on Christmas Eve, when the astronauts were circling the moon, they took an iconic picture of the earth. No one had ever seen a picture of earth from such a long distance. Earth looked so small and vulnerable.

"In 1914 with a war raging on Christmas Eve, a British soldier heard something he had never heard before.

The Germans were singing. He knew the tune, but not the words. When they stopped singing, their foes applauded them and then replied by singing the English version of *Silent Night.* On Christmas morning both sides spilled out of their trenches and walked toward one another, wishing each other a Merry Christmas. They exchanged gifts, and some even played soccer, and later they went back to war.

"Tonight, this might be the most significant Christmas ever, because if you believe that Jesus came to earth for you, Christmas will be great."

Nikki got lost in the remainder of the message, remembering the ache she had in her heart when she renounced God for taking her husband from her. The message was really coming through loud and clear from the pastor with the southern twang. She nodded her head, getting it, and it was good.

Marnie talked about what was coming up in January, but she said that "this will be your best Christmas ever if you take Jesus into your heart. Soon we're going to light candles and sing *Silent Night.* This year is the 200th anniversary of the hymn. The writer wanted this new song to be accompanied with the church organ, but it wasn't functioning. Instead the first time the song was played and sung it was on a guitar.

Marnie continued talking about Jesus and what He knows about us, and that He came for us at Christmas. "Back in 2000, Peter Jennings was hosting a show called Searching for Jesus." He opened the show by saying, 'Good evening, I'm Peter Jennings, and we've been searching for Jesus as reporters, that is, because it's an irrestible story, and whatever your faith or religion, there's simply no denying the extraordinary influence that Jesus has had and that He does have in our lives.

"Tonight, can be the most important Christmas Eve of your life if you do the search, if you'll take the steps to Jesus. If you'll do it tonight, I promise you'll never regret it." She ended with a prayer.

Christmas, December 25th, 2018

1

At 5:30 AM her iPhone vibrated. Sara McGinnis lifted it from the nightstand and offered a sleepy "Hello."

After listening for a minute, she pressed 'End' and placed the phone back on the nightstand. She slipped out of bed, hurried to the bathroom, and peed as the shower water warmed up. Sara took a quick shower, dried off, pulled on her underpants, slipped into a bra, and went back out to the bedroom. She looked over at Mike who was snoring like a buzz saw and then donned a fresh uniform. She put on her socks and shoes and gave Mike a peck on the cheek. After a quick cup of coffee and a slice of buttered toast, she went outside, hopped in her car and was on her way to the station. Officer Tony Wilkes had been admitted to St. Luke's Hospital for an emergency appendectomy, and she was scheduled to take his shift. Sara did not like working on Christmas, but she knew the possibility always loomed, even if married to the chief.

Sara drove down a nearly deserted Main Street where, less than twelve hours ago, shoppers were still looking for that last minute gift or grabbing a nice meal at one of the downtown restaurants. She looked up and saw the word HOTEL on the top of the *Hotel Bethlehem* was turned off, but BETHLEHEM shone brightly, welcoming travelers to the Christmas City. She passed by Brian and Jessie Miller's house, seeing all the white Christmas lights and candles still lit up. Their house was gorgeous, and she couldn't wait to stop by after work for the open house the Millers were hosting. She shook her head, wondering why Brian was still delivering mail after coming into all that money. Brian was actually standing on his front porch, so she stopped and opened the passenger window, shouting, "Merry Christmas, Brian."

He saw it was Sara, and he quickly stepped off his porch and ambled down to her car. He saw her in full uniform and said, "Got called in, did ya?"

She nodded. "If all goes well, I should be finished by 3:30 and then Mike and I will be here around 5."

"No problem, Sara. I know what is like to be called in, although not on a holiday, but it sure messes up your schedule for that day."

"True." She smiled. "Okay, I better get to work and keep crime in check. Later, my friend."

He replied, "Later," as the window worked its way upward.

A half hour later she was sitting in a patrol car alongside rookie Lewis Gates. She liked Lewis, but he still had an awful lot to learn. Today would probably be a good day to test his knowledge, she thought. Hopefully that would help make the day go faster.

2

Still in their jammies, Julian and Petra padded down the stairs. The scent of coffee called them to the kitchen, and after pouring cups, they strolled into the living room. The TV was showing Bob Hope, obviously at one of his Vietnam Christmas shows, while Riley slept on the hearth in front of the fireplace. Brian was sitting in his reclining chair, a lap table resting on him as he was coloring a picture in a rather large coloring book.

He heard the couple walk in, and Riley's head came up and his tail wagged when he saw his master and Petra. Riley stood up and stretched, then he rubbed against

Julian's leg. Julian pulled a treat from his pocket and handed it to the dog.

"Morning, folks. Merry Christmas," Brian said, not raising his head as he selected another crayon from the large 64 Crayola crayon box.

Julian strolled over to him and lifted one side of the coloring book up to see the cover. "A Colonial Coloring Book? This seems rather old judging from the browning of the pages I see." He laid the book flat on the table.

"It is rather old, Julian. I have loved to color since I was a kid. My mom and dad taught me how to move the crayon in a circular pattern, and to stay in the lines. I bought this coloring book many years ago on a trip to Williamsburg, but I lost it somewhere along the line. A couple of years ago I had the desire to try and find a copy. I looked on eBay and a couple of days and nearly nineteen dollars later, I had the book again. The original price was marked on the cover-sixty-nine cents. The pages have indeed yellowed, or perhaps browned, but when I apply color, the patina seems richer. I like it."

Petra said, "I love to color, too, Doc. Would you allow me the honor of doing a page before we have to leave? Also, I see you sign and date each finished page. Did your parents teach you that, as well?"

"They did. You certainly may color a page before you guys leave. I don't know about you two, but I am ready to open my presents!"

Julian and Petra nodded, and Riley danced as they gathered on the floor by the tree.

3

Angela was excited. She concluded her $500 shopping spree yesterday afternoon, giving Al and Lon time to open some of the boxes and put the toys, memorabilia, and games on the display shelves.

When she had entered the store yesterday, she was overwhelmed by the amount of really neat things that she saw. There were so many different types of things from the past, none of them being electronic, except for a toy called Electric Football. Figuring her brother, Jose might like that, she made it her first choice. One display case caught her eye. Her brother was a baseball fanatic, and he knew many stats from players dating back to the early years of the game. She studied the baseball cards and thought the prices were too high, not knowing the value of some of the cardboard pictures. There were a couple of sealed boxes, much like decks of cards, with fifteen cards in each box. She decided to take two boxes.

Angela purchased a Slinky toy, a Fort Apache set, several puzzles and games, and a framed 11 x 14 photo of the 1950 Philadelphia Phillies-The Whiz Kids.

Later, at home, she was sitting on a stuffed pillow on the floor near the space heater, because she was a little cold. For Christmas the temperature was relatively warm, and she had wanted a white Christmas so badly. This Christmas could be Jose's last according to what the doctor told her mom on the phone around Thanksgiving. She wanted this to be his happiest Christmas ever.

When he wheeled himself into the living room and saw all the gifts beneath the tree, many for him, he was ecstatic and almost fell off his chair in a rush to begin opening the packages.

He opened the box that held the two small boxes of baseball cards, pulling each card out very gently, one at a time. The first card was of Hank Aaron, next was Rollie Fingers, but the third one made him shake. "Mom, can you look something up on the computer for me, please?" He told her what to keyword and when the page came up, she cried out. "Jose, Angela, many of our prayers have been answered with this card. This Mickey Mantle rookie card from 1951 could be valued at as much as one million dollars. If Jose lets me find a buyer, I would be very happy."

"Of course, Mama, you may sell it. A million dollars is a lot of money. You could pay off all our bills and maybe get us a nice, little house with a back yard."

They were so excited, he didn't even open the other box of cards, but when he would, later that day, there would be another valuable card with the image of Babe Ruth.

4

After Lon Seager closed their store, *Retro,* yesterday at 6 PM, he added up the receipts and was blown away with how much people spent during the day. The *Bethlehem News* had printed a lengthy story about the shop, and especially the hula hoop contest. The piece went viral on the Internet and several Pennsylvania newspapers carried the story.

During the day, he had to open many of the cartons, not even knowing what was in them. Customers were buying everything they saw. The activity in the store seemed nearly magical.

In one day alone, there were sales of over thirty-seven thousand dollars. Not only would the store survive through the remainder of the year, the boom would continue into 2022 until another slowdown in the economy occurred. Over those years, Al and Lon both searched online to try to come up with another store selling retro toys and games, to buy their inventory, but those stores were finally coming back to life again.

Manufacturers in the United States were getting in on the phenomenon of remaking some of the old-time toys because their popularity had gone through the roof. Kids were beginning to play with classic toys again.

Then they finally found a store that was willing to part with all their stuff.

5

Sara and Lewis were enjoying a very easy day of patrolling. Lewis was so happy that she was taking time to teach him the many things he would have to know about being a cop in Bethlehem.

Just around noon they decided to take a lunch break, and they chose the *Hotel Bethlehem*. Sara had called the hotel manager, Dennis Costello, to see if they would be able to get a table. "Of course, Sara. I actually will have a table available at the front window in the Tap Room." When they arrived, the two cops sat down. Each of them ordered a burger, fries, and diet Cokes. Sara really would have liked to drink a beer with her lunch, but that was a no-no, especially for the wife of the chief of police.

After popping a couple of fries in his mouth and chewing them up, Lewis said, "Sara, is being married to the chief a pain in the ass sometimes?"

She laughed. "It sure is, Lewis. Mike and I were partners when the vampire was roaming Bethlehem, and we really had each other's backs. I miss riding with him, but I know he definitely deserved the promotion. He has busted his butt for all the years he's been on the force. I get a lot of teasing, a lot like Eddie gets about her relationship with Jamie on *Blue Bloods*. I've gotten used to it, though even though it has only been a short period of time since he got the job. I don't know what the brass says to him, but I'm sure he takes a good bit of friendly ball busting."

"I want to thank you again for all you've been teaching me today. I want to be a good cop because there have been many law enforcement officers on my family tree. My great-great, whatever grandfather was a detective in Philly in the 1860's and he was assigned to be a guard on Lincoln's funeral train. That was quite an honor."

"Wow, Lewis, that sure was an honor."

They stepped out onto the street and walked up to the patrol car parked about a block away, where they were greeted with a couple of rounds from a handgun. Their guns were drawn, and their eyes were searching for the shooter before the third round was fired. Lewis saw the man in a combat crouch, and he threw his body in front of Sara, getting hit in the left arm but saving her from getting hit.

Sara reacted quickly, snapping off two shots, both hitting the man although they did not produce serious wounds. She quickly raced to the man and wrested the gun from his hand, pushing him to the sidewalk and cuffing him in several quick motions. "Shots fired, officer down, between 8 and 12 West Broad. Shooter is cuffed, but he is wounded. Send a unit and an ambulance."

After cuffing the perp, she hurried back to check on Lewis. He was holding his arm, and waving her off, signifying that he was going to be okay, but she checked out his wound before heading back to the shooter. She had been able to keep an eye on him as she checked out her partner.

"Sit up, and face me," she ordered the man, then she saw that it was Randall Burton, the Santa porch pirate she arrested four days ago. "How the hell are you out of jail and were you stalking me, you piece of crap?"

"I made bail." He spat on the sidewalk, just missing her highly polished shoes. "I've been watching for you ever since, because after arresting me and then that story by the paper, I've become a laughingstock with my homeless friends. I told myself a long time ago that if anyone made me a laughingstock, I'd get them. You're lucky you have a quick partner, or there would have been a big hole in your head, bitch."

The ambulance arrived shortly after two patrol cars. The two wounded men were loaded in the back, along with a police guard, while the remaining cops talked to Sara.

She was leaning against a car as the adrenalin rushed through her system. And she was happy to be alive.

She called Mike to tell him what had just gone down.

6

Russ Gallagher was not too far away when he heard the pops, identifying them as shots fired from more than one handgun. He raced toward the sound, being careful not to get into any line of fire because the best time to report a story was in the moments after the action occurred.

He saw two police officers in a shootout with a lone gunman who went down a moment later. As he arrived across the street, Sara McGinnis was cuffing the man. He recognized him as the package thief. He spotted the other police officer, holding his arm and he could see blood dripping between his fingers. Sara appeared not to have been hit, and he was very glad for that. Mike would have crapped a brick if his wife would have been wounded, and God save the person who would kill her, because Mike would get that perp somehow.

After Burton was on his way to the hospital, Russ crossed the street to comfort Sara.

"Sara, are you okay?" He inquired, hugging her.

She nodded and looked up at him, tears streaming down his face. "If Lewis hadn't seen him first..." She took a moment to compose herself. "I think I would be headed to the morgue as we speak. That gun appeared so big, and he looked like he was right in my face instead of a couple of yards away. I sure got lucky. Fortunately, Lewis will be okay, and he'll have a story to tell his kids and grandkids someday." Her cell phone rang, and she answered it, stepping a few paces away from Russ.

When she returned to him, she told him that Mike got the word and he's glad that I'm fine and that Lewis will be okay as well. "He'll see you at Brian's party, later."

"I'm looking forward to that. Hearing everyone's Christmas stories will be fun. The nice thing about that is that all the guests will have their stories written down, and Brian will send them all to everybody's email addresses. I might have a pretty good little article from those stories. Alright, I'll see you later. I guess you will be finished with patrolling for the day?"

"Yeah, sadly that will mean one less patrol on the street, but its Christmas Day, what could happen?" She laughed and threw her hands up in the air.

7

Brian and Jessie had opened their presents to each other early in the morning while drinking coffee, after a great breakfast of pancakes, Spam, and eggs. They figured they wouldn't have lunch because once the open house started at three, there would be a great deal of drinking and nibbling.

There was some last-minute cleaning to do, mostly straightening up, and Brian oversaw those duties. The after-party cleaning would be fun tomorrow. He would be on vacation until January 3rd. Jessie got him a brand-new Shark Rotator vacuum cleaner for Christmas, and he was anxious to try it out. House cleaning really calmed him down, and he used his day off to perform those chores. If he had to work his day off, he did the vacuuming on Sunday after church until his favorite team, or golfer, came on and then finished before dinner.

They had no idea how many people were going to pop in. Nine people received written invitations, but he told everyone at the post office to come by for a drink, and Jessie let all her friends know via email. They had been thinking about creating an Open House Facebook page but thought the amount of people reading it and deciding to stop by would be more than overwhelming.

He looked out the window and saw Julian and Petra Ross taking Riley for a stroll. He was pretty sure he liked them both but creating long-distance friendships didn't always pan out. Brian Kethledge was a very good friend to them, and he told them about their immortality. Doc felt that he could trust the Millers with their secret, and he would never be proven wrong on that.

He was hoping that many of the attendees would share a Christmas story, and he was going to read one out loud. The story was written by a retired Allentown city carrier, and he told about his first Christmas Eve with the Post Office.

8

Hyram and Susan spent a long, leisurely time in bed, resting up after the long holiday season shopping season. Their shop was busy nearly every day, and they already had enough money saved up to visit their friends at Wrightsville Beach for two weeks, beginning May 18th.

Steve and Mary Wright's apartment was going to be available, and before they headed back to Pennsylvania last spring, they had asked the Wrights if they could stay there in 2019. There was a discouraging time when Hurricane Florence made landfall near the old house in September. A couple of days later, Hy called Steve and found out that there was minimal damage, and they were able to reopen for the final few weeks of this past season.

He was certainly hoping that there would be no paranormal activity going on, allowing Susan and him to have an enjoyable two weeks. There were so many restaurants they wanted to try; however, one of their favorites, *Causeway Café* had closed their doors last month. Dave Monaghan owned the restaurant for thirty-five years and decided to retire. Susan was really devastated when Hy told her the news, hoping that someone would buy the building and reopen it. Dave and his chefs served up the best shrimp and grits in the area.

So much had happened to them in the last eight years: slaying vampires, destroying werewolves and their clones, eliminating spirits, changing evil witches to good, and killing more werewolf clones in Wilmington, North Carolina. These were challenges that no man or woman should ever have to encounter.

They were both looking forward to spending quality time with the Millers. Brian and Jessie were both Christmas fanatics and the outside of their historic home was elegantly gorgeous with mainly white lights. They had found a manger scene in an old barn in New York and couldn't wait to set it up on their front yard. The artwork on the faces of Mary, Joseph and Jesus appeared so lifelike that he and Susan stared at it for a long time when they walked by a couple of days ago.

For the remainder of Christmas Day, they planned to only read the paper, watch a couple of more *Hallmark* movies and eat a light lunch, saving lots of room for all the goodies that would be found on tables at the Millers.

Christmas Day-The Open House

1

The sign board on the porch read *IF YOU ARE A FRIEND, THIS DOOR IS OPEN TO YOU. IF YOU HAVE A CHRISTMAS STORY YOU WOULD LIKE TO SHARE, THIS DOOR IS OPEN TO YOU. MERRY CHRISTMAS AND WELCOME TO OUR HOME.*

Hyram and Susan read the sign and stepped inside. A fire was crackling in the large fireplace that was the focal point of the house's entry. Fresh greens and scented candles offered a freshness to the air as soft Christmas music played through hidden speakers. The eight-foot-tall Christmas tree was gorgeously decorated, colorfully wrapped presents still lying on the tree skirt beneath the majestic Douglas Fir.

Guests were seated on the comfortable furniture along with card table chairs. Keeping those people in rapt attention with a smattering of laughter was Roy Clayton, retired mailman and regionally famous author.

"...so, I went downstairs to answer the doorbell and when I opened the door, nobody was there. Baffled, I climbed back up the stairs to the living room. Riley was sitting on his haunches at the balcony door, and he had an 'I'm sorry' look on his face. I couldn't imagine that he could have caused or gotten into any trouble in the short period of time he was out of my sight. Well, I was wrong. I turned toward the living room and stared at the coffee table. My beautifully crafted ham and cheese sandwich had disappeared.

"I turned to my faithful dog and asked, 'Riley, did you eat my lunch?' His tongue came out and he licked his mouth-a dead giveaway to being the sandwich criminal. I gave him a bit of a tongue lashing and told him I wasn't going to speak to him for the rest of the day.

"When the boss," pointing to his wife, Susan, "came home, I told her what happened. 'Roy, you know he forgot about what he did, even before your lunch in his belly was digested. Give your puppy a hug, scratch his ears and love him. The poor dog was hungry, and you lost, dear" He saw her laugh along with the crowd listening to his story. "What could I do, folks? I gave him some loving and then we were both happy."

Roy saw Hy and Susan, gave them a wave, took a healthy pull from his beer, and began another story, this one about his mail-carrying days. He used to say, 'Damn, I wish I would have written down all the stories and one-liners said on the job for almost thirty years. I could have written that book very easily.'

Finished with his stories, he rose from the chair, and a woman immediately took over the conversation.

2

"Hi, everyone, and Merry Christmas. I'm Karen Samuels, a resident of Bethlehem, and I come from a family of schoolteachers. Through the years at family gatherings, I heard many stories from those in the education field about how their students were terrific, challenging, entertaining or in sad situations. My mother, a sixth grade English teacher in Allentown, told the following story to us about a teacher with whom she once worked. The two visits in the story take place on December 26th, twenty years apart."

"I'm here to visit your patient, Kathleen O'Sullivan. My name is Dr. Joseph Scott. I called ahead." The nurse at the desk gave me barely a glance and said, "Yes Doctor, we were expecting you. Kathy is in room 108, just down the hall on your right." Well-worn Christmas decorations were scattered along the walls surrounding the desk, waiting room and lobby. I noticed as I walked toward room 108 that the decorations didn't make it as far as the halls or patient rooms. I reached Mrs. O'Sullivan's room or, as I knew her as a student, "Miss Murphy." The door was open revealing a thin, gray-haired version of the Miss Murphy I remembered. She was sitting in the only chair in the room and gazing out the window. I knocked on the door, even though it was open, to receive her permission to enter the room. The knock startled her, but her inquiring look brought me right back to sixth grade. There she was, Miss Murphy, my sixth grade English teacher, whose sharp eyes never missed a thing.

After we established that Mrs. O'Sullivan remembered me, I asked if I could visit and sit on her bed. I wondered about the other bed in the room, "Mrs. O'Sullivan, do you have a roommate?"

"Yes. My roommate, Lori, is in physical therapy now. She suffered a stroke which left her with no speech and no movement on her left side. Poor woman."

I took a look at the dreary room décor, stains on the mustard colored rug, the dingy white walls, and lack of personal photos or memorabilia. A sudden racket in the hall prompted Mrs. O'Sullivan to stand up and quickly close the door. When she returned to her chair, I inquired, "Mrs. O'Sullivan, how did you come to live here, if you don't mind my asking?"

She replied, "Joe, I am so proud of your success. Do you mind if I call you Joe? Please call me Kathy. We are many years beyond our student-teacher relationship. I came to this nursing home to be close to my husband Jack as he recovered from a hip replacement just after he retired as a transportation administrator for the Saucon Valley

School District. Sadly, his pain from the operation disguised a malignant tumor on his bladder. By the time his surgeon discovered the cancer, it had spread to his other organs. He died three years ago in this facility. We went through all our savings to pay for his care."

"Kathy, do you have any medical problems?"

"No, just the normal stuff that comes with aging. I get along fine. My son George calls me every few weeks. He is a professor of literature at Berkeley College in California."

Overwhelmed by her dismal living arrangements I asked Kathy "It is none of my business, but wouldn't you prefer to live near your son? I live in Mill Valley which is close to Berkeley and the weather there is mild. It is a beautiful area with lots to do."

Kathy considered the question for a moment and replied, "Well, I think my son needs his independence. He went through a difficult time as a teenager after he told us he was gay. I did everything I could to convince Jack to accept George for whom he was but to his final breath, he refused to speak to his son. George knows I love him unconditionally. Besides, I have no money to move, and I do not want to be a burden on George. It makes me happy that he finally has a comfortable life with good friends. That is enough about me. Tell me about you, Joe. Your mother has kept in touch with me every Christmas. I know the broad strokes about your medical degree, your lovely wife and three daughters."

"Kathy, as you know I had some problems during my childhood. I am in Allentown now to spend some time with my mother who is recovering from a knee replacement. She is doing well and has a home health aide that comes daily. For old times' sake I bought a fresh live tree and decorated it for her. To celebrate we had sugar cookies from the Hellertown Bakery and hot chocolate, just like the old days.

We have been doing a lot of reminiscing and I learned that there was one event during Christmas break when I was in sixth grade that changed our family's lives.

"A person took notice of my sadness and visited my mother. That person acted in a way my mother was incapable of at the time. She arranged for my father to be hospitalized in a rehabilitation program. He returned to us as the dad I loved, and he remained sober for the rest of his life. As unlikely as it seems, he was welcomed back to his old job as an auto mechanic. My mother believes that our turn of fortune was all due to the efforts of one woman, my sixth grade English teacher. I heard this story for the first time yesterday, and I had to come to see you to thank you."

Kathy's eyes were downcast. The surrounding nursing home sounds suddenly became more noticeable as she pondered what he said. Finally, she softly said, "I could never turn my back on a student who was suffering through no fault of his or her own. Yours was a loving family who was strong enough to make it with a little help. It was my pleasure."

At that moment an aide returned, who briskly announced that visiting hours were over, and pushed Kathy's roommate in a wheelchair into the room. The teacher and student said their goodbyes with promises to keep in touch.

A few days later the phone in Kathy's room rang. Upon answering it, Kathy was delighted to hear her son George's voice on the other end.

He said, "Mom I had a visitor, someone you taught at Raub Middle School, Joe Scott. We talked for a long time. I have been considering this for a while... I want you to visit me in Berkeley to think over if you would like to move out here permanently. I booked a flight to Allentown for this

Saturday to discuss this in person. I feel that you will love it here as much as I do."

After no response from Kathy, George asked, "Mom! Are you there? Have I upset you?"

Kathy emitted a small sob and said, "Yes, I want to move to Berkeley and be more a part of your life. I want to meet your friends and students. I'll start packing now!"

My mother learned through a Christmas card from Kathy that she is living in an apartment in Berkeley, around the corner from her son's home. She is certified as an English as a Second Language teacher and works with children of migrants working in California. Kathy also sees her student Joe and his family, usually on December 26th. Joe's daughters beg Kathy for stories about their father as a young boy. She tells the girls that he was the smartest, sweetest student that a teacher could ever want. Joe addressed his daughters, "Girls someday you will look back on your years in school and realize there was that one teacher who made a lasting positive impact on your life. For me, it was Mrs. Kathleen O'Sullivan."

3

Neither host was available after Karen concluded her story. Heads turned from side to side, wondering if Brian or Jessie had picked who should go next.

Sara stood up and said, "Brian and Jessie will be incommunicado for a few minutes. Brian asked if I could have Mike tell you all about his brother Jack. It is a sad Christmas story, for sure, but I think he would like to share it with you." She looked toward her husband and said, "Mike?"

He nodded, but everyone could already see the sadness growing on his face and the lump that came to his throat before he even uttered a sound. He took the proffered chair that the other story tellers had sat in and took a seat.

"Back in 2010 the city was facing a paranormal threat in the guise of a vampire. If you haven't heard about it, you probably were under a rock at that time." He smiled, garnering a modicum of laughter. "My partner and I were sent to break up a street fight; and when we took them to the station, I took one of the fighters into an interview room. The man was my older brother, Jack, a Marine who was only a couple of years away from retirement. I ripped him a new one for fighting with a Muslim

"Until that day I had not seen my brother for twenty years. When he left, my mom was devastated. Jack was strong and popular. He had good grades and was a star football player. At a Thanksgiving Day game, he intercepted a pass and ran it back eighty-nine yards for a touchdown to win the game. He told me he had to leave; because after our dad died, Mom expected him to be the man of the house, and he just wasn't ready for that kind of responsibility. He left, and we never heard from him again.

"We were almost dead broke, and with Jack gone there was no extra income he could have brought in working a summer job. I was just a kid and couldn't help financially until I picked up two paper routes the following year. That helped somewhat.

"He didn't realize how rough it was without him. Our aunt Jennie helped us out by giving Mom enough money to pay off the house. Once I went to work full-time, I gave her money every month until the 'loan' was paid off."

He saw Sara walk to the kitchen, probably to bring some more trays of food to the guests.

"Jack told me he became a Marine and how tough boot camp was. He became a sniper and picked off a Taliban

137

soldier at two thousand yards, which is impressive shooting. He was just in one of his moods when he saw the Muslim and went ballistic. I know that has happened to World War Two vets when they saw Japanese people and to Korea and Vietnam vets as well. However, that certainly didn't give Jack the right to start beating up on the man.

"Long story short, the Muslim man gave us a number in dollars that would make this go away. Jack really wanted to be able to retire, but this incident could have finished him. It cost me ten grand, but he was my brother after all.

"Jack hung out with us and helped slay the vampire before heading back to duty. About a month later he was in Afghanistan and was reported missing and then after about a year, the Marines declared him dead. It really got to Mom, and she died the following year, not able to fight her cancer any longer.

"Although I love Christmas, I am always saddened, knowing I will never see my brother again."

Mike began to sob and then felt a hand on his shoulder. He looked up and stared at the face of his brother, Jack.

4

Master Gunnery Sergeant Jack McGinnis, after a long round of hugs and tears, sat in the chair to tell his story. Mike McGinnis pulled up a chair beside him, wanting to be as close to his brother as possible after thinking him dead for so long.

"I don't quite know where to begin because much of what I was doing was, and still is, considered top secret. I was enlisted to go on a mission in the mountains of Afghanistan to execute a high-ranking leader. That's about all I can give you about the mission, but I can tell you what happened to me, and why I was gone for so long.

"We were a team of three utilizing weapons, uniforms, and rations that were untraceable to any American manufacturer. We were not allowed to take any identification with us at all, and all our dog tags had on them were our dates of birth and blood type, in Cyrillic. I did a lot of sneaky Pete ops in my career, but never one as tightly structured as this one.

"It took us nearly four days, traveling only under the cover of darkness, to reach our destination. Once there we dug very shallow fighting holes, and I studied my line of fire to where the target was supposed to be. The target, and I can't tell you whether it was a male or female, would be meeting with other leaders of the Taliban. The target was to be accompanied by forty tough rebels. I would probably only get off one shot before they would attack our position. Even if my shot was successful and eliminated the target, we'd be in a world of hurt. We did find some places to hide on our trip to the site but getting there without getting our asses shot off would be a tough gig.

"The next morning, actually closer to noon, the entourage appeared. My target was visible almost immediately after their arrival. I took my shot, blowing off the target's head, and the race for survival was on.

"We immediately came under withering fire as we took off for the hiding spot we hoped to find. As we ran, I stumbled and fell in a ravine. I told my team members to leave me and save themselves, as I quickly gathered brush to cover myself and blend into the landscape. My camouflage worked, but about ten minutes later I heard the firing of many automatic weapons, and I figured my men were dead.

"At nightfall I headed east, toward Pakistan, and I was able to walk for three days. On the third day I was on a ridge just above a small village. I was out of water and only had a package of beef jerky left. After reconnoitering the ville for most of the day, only seeing old men, women and children, I decided to see if I could dig up some food and water and, hopefully, continue on my merry way.

"Coming down the ridge, I twisted my ankle and fell ass over tin can into the valley below. Excuse me a moment please.

While Jack took his break, Russ and Joanne Gallagher strolled into the house, carrying several bottles of wine and a cheese plate. Once introductions were made, they found a couple of empty seats and sat down.

5

After relieving himself and grabbing some food and a beer, Jack sat back down in the chair and continued his story.

"From that moment on, until a couple of weeks ago, I couldn't remember who I was, where I was, what I was doing, and, well, nothing. It took a couple of days before I could walk properly, and by then I realized that there were no young men in the village. I helped out with all the chores, I rebuilt many of their broken-down buildings, dug a well, and more than I could ever remember.

"When my memory returned, I bid those people goodbye and worked my way back to American lines. I reported in, was debriefed for several days, and told that I would be sent home. I asked them not to contact Mike because I wanted to surprise him. They told me he had recently become Chief of Police in Bethlehem, and I felt so proud. I was also told that my mom had passed almost five years ago and that saddened me deeply.

"When I arrived in Bethlehem early this morning, I found out about this very cool party and thought that now would be a good time to surprise my brother. I never want to be apart from him and the rest of my family ever."

"Master Gunny, can I ask you a question?" Jessie Miller said.

"Sure, but only if you call me Jack."

She nodded. "Jack, are you still planning on retiring?"

"Actually, I'm not. I was going to tell Mike and Sara later, but now is as good a time as any. I was asked to serve as the first sergeant for a training battalion at Quantico, Virginia. They are guaranteeing me to stay there for two years until I get my thirty years in. I thought it was a good deal, so I took it. I'll be able to visit Mike and Sara more frequently, and they could also come and see me."

Brian Kethledge raised his hand. "May I assume you are going to be receiving all your back pay, and can you tell me if your team members were brought home?"

"Yes, I received all my back pay, but my buddies did not come home because of the nature of the mission. I certainly hope that someday they will be laid to rest in America, but the odds are really slim.

"Thanks for the questions. Merry Christmas."

6

"I know this story of a worst Christmas is not anywhere near as bad as Mike's or Jack's but when you are a kid, things seem much worse than they are. My name is Robert Green, and like others here, I am a Vietnam veteran, having served fourteen months, the additional time allowing me to separate from the service early. I was a company clerk with the 510th Signal Company in Cam Ranh Bay in 1970 and 1971.

"I think it was 1955 and Christmas fell on a Sunday that year. My brother and I were going to get bikes as Christmas gifts because we sneaked down to the cellar one day and saw them against a wall, covered with tarps. We figured our folks probably bought them at Guy's Hardware on Main Street in Slatington. I mentioned this because back in those days people shopped in their hometowns or nearby, giving local stores the business. The store celebrated its 150th anniversary last year.

"When we woke up on Christmas morning, there were two issues that were going to stop me from riding my bike. It had snowed heavily overnight, and the plows didn't come through too frequently back in the day, especially on a weekend. I also woke up sick as a dog. I was vomiting and had horrific diarrhea. My parents called Doctor Harry Kern, our local doc, to come over and check me out. Back then, a lot of family doctors made house calls.

"To make matters worse later in the day, the snow turned to rain and the rain turned to slush. Later in the week it started to get warmer, I got well because of the care from "Doc Harry," the snow melted away, and before school started again, my brother Bill and I started to ride our bikes. It was a while before the training wheels came off. I have had a bicycle ever since, and I still like to ride when I can. But I will never forget the Christmas that I spent in bed, not knowing which end to hang over the toilet."

7

Nikki Lawson and her husband, Larry, finally arrived. His plane was late getting in.

142

Although Nikki knew several people in the house, Larry knew no one. That was resolved in a few minutes when Nikki introduced him to everyone she knew and those who were just there to mainly tell their stories introduced themselves.

She got everyone's attention and told them all her backstory up until she left Bethlehem. She grew quiet for several long moments and then began. "After losing Chuck, I knew I had to get away from here, so I packed a few belongings, leaving the rest for my folks to deal with; and I hopped in the car, heading west. I didn't know where I would wind up, but I had almost six thousand dollars in cash and checking, and three credit cards worth nearly fifteen grand.

"I drove for about ten hours the first day, winding up in Indiana. I rented a room for the evening. I had dinner at a nice restaurant, and on the way back to my hotel I spotted a liquor store and bought a bottle of Jack to help me pass the night or pass out. I didn't really care which one would happen.

"Sleep came and went. Every time I woke up, I took a belt of Jack and waited for the alcohol to make me drowsy. If it didn't work in five or ten minutes, Jack would need to help me out again. I don't remember when I drifted off, but when I woke up, my iPhone read 10:45. A terrible odor assaulted my nostrils. I had peed and crapped while I was in bed, not able to hold my bladder or bowels. I took a shower and washed the sheets in the bathtub, hanging them up for the maid service. I was so embarrassed, I left her twenty bucks for a tip.

"I had just crossed into Iowa when the engine light went on. Fortunately, I was only about a mile from a service center. An attendant looked at it and said, 'This make, and model is prevalent to having the light come on because of vapor getting trapped by the gas cap. Chances are that's all that it is, but the garage is closed. If you bring it by at seven AM, someone will be here to take a look at it. Hopefully you'll be on your way not long after.'

"At seven a mechanic looked at it and put the diagnostic tester to work. What you were told last night is true. You won't have any trouble getting to where you're going, but someday you should have someone inspect it." I thanked him, handed him a twenty for his time and began heading west again.

"Late in the afternoon the car began sputtering, and it shut down on me. I was able to pull off to the side of the road and I put the hood up, hoping someone would come to my aid. I really had no idea what was wrong with the damn car now, but it wouldn't start.

"About a half hour later a car pulled over and a handsome, young man started walking my way. 'Hi, Miss. I'll save you the redneck joke by saying you do seem to have a car problem. What can you tell me and maybe I can help you out? I have had some experience working on cars.'

"After explaining my problem, he went back to his pickup truck and returned with a long flexible metal rod. He opened the gas cap and ran the rod down to the bottom of the tank and when he ran his fingers over it, it was dry as a bone. 'When's the last time you got gas? Your tank is empty.'

"Oh my God, I forgot to get gas when I was at the service station this morning getting the car checked out. I am such an idiot."

"He said, 'I live about twenty miles from here. It's a small town called Emmaus. We have one bar, one restaurant, one church, and one gas station. I'll have the owner Mark Tydell tow your car tomorrow and he'll fill your tank and check out your engine light problem. If he can't fix it, at least you should be able to get to your destination.'

"We got into his pickup truck, and I turned toward him to tell him that I grew up in Emmaus, Pennsylvania." The dome light was on because he hadn't yet closed his door all the way. It was then I noticed his burgundy clergy shirt with the white-collar tab. 'You're a priest?' I inquired.

"'No,' he replied, closing the door, which turned off the light. 'I'm the pastor of Emmaus Bethlehem Lutheran Church.'

"I laughed. Actually, it was probably a cackle which caught him off guard. 'I have a long story to tell you, but right now I'll tell you that I am from Emmaus, I was a cop in Bethlehem, and I have renounced God. *Of course* I would run into a pastor in Iowa.'

"I'm going to have Larry continue with the story, now."

8

"I was taken aback when Nikki told me she had renounced God. I had only been a pastor for a little over a year when we met, and I had never run into that before and, may I say, since. She told me what had happened to make her abandon our Lord and Savior. We talked all the way back to Emmaus, and then I invited her to my house for dinner and more talk.

"We talked for hours and then she stayed in the guest room, telling me in the morning that she hadn't slept at all, and she'd picked up the Bible on the nightstand and skimmed through it, taking notes and asking me many questions at breakfast.

"After her car was towed to the garage, Mark filled the tank and checked the engine light problem. He happened to have a gas cap to replace the bad one, and the engine light went off. Problem solved.

"While we waited, I showed her around town. We were in the police station when I received a call from a parishioner, and I had to return to the church to talk to him.

"About an hour later I returned to the station and I saw Nikki sitting at a desk, typing onto a laptop computer. She looked up from her project and said, 'I've accomplished a lot in the time you were gone. I saw a note on the bulletin board that the police station was looking for a secretary, one that had police experience. I told them about myself and now I'm filling out the application. I also found out that there is a furnished one-bedroom apartment available, so I called the landlord and I got that. I've been doing a lot of soul searching since I met you and I've concluded that I was sent here by God to get myself straightened out and to make this place my home.'

"I counseled Nikki for months, and she came to worship every Sunday. We had come to know each other so well. After she had lived there for almost a year, Nikki and I began dating and we married this past July. The coolest thing about that was when the JP said, 'Do you, Nikki Lawson, take this man, Larry Lawson, to be your lawfully wedded husband?'

The guests exploded in applause.

9

A woman with a huge smile sat in the chair. "Hi folks. I'm Christine Held, and I am an author writing under the name of Christina Paul. I have published four books and one of my books, *Second Chance,* was awarded best romance novel in the 2013 Indie Next Generation Book Awards. I'm a friend of Roy Clayton, and he invited me to visit him this

Christmas. I live in Hillsborough, New Jersey. Roy was a member of an author's group I once ran.

"In July of 1984, I moved out of my parents' house and into my first apartment. I was going to school full-time and working full-time. Money was tight, to say the least, but every extra cent went to buy presents for Christmas that year. I was even measuring wrapping paper to the exact size so as not to waste a scrap. I didn't even have anything extra to decorate my apartment, and I certainly could not afford a tree.

"On December 23rd, I came home a little before midnight. The retail store I worked at closed at eleven PM. When I walked in, the apartment had a strange glow. While I was at work, Paul, my late husband, who was then my boyfriend, had bought a tree, decorated it, and then decorated the whole apartment. He had even hung a Christmas dish towel from the stove.

"That night I slept on the living room floor under the tree. Paul couldn't have given me a better Christmas present if he had tried.

10

When the door opened, Riley raced inside, jumping on Brian Kethledge's lap, giving him a couple of big licks. Laughter broke out among the guests, and the little brown and white dog just kept kissing the white-haired man. Before too long saliva was dripping down the man's beard onto his shirt, until a voice said, "'Nuf, Ri."

The dog jumped from Brian's lap and sauntered over to Julian and Petra Ross, licking the man's hand. Julian was carrying a red bag filled with gifts. He took the bag from his shoulder and placed it on the floor. Roy Clayton had just stepped into the room and stared at the dog for a very long minute, and then he shouted, "Riley, you've come back to me, boy!" He got down on one knee and the dog strolled over to him and began licking his face.

He looked up at the man and woman, saying, "I'm sorry for my outburst, but your dog looks just like my late Riley"

"That's okay, Mister. My dog is named Riley, too."

"What a coincidence! You see, I lost Riley almost four years ago, and I pray to God every night that He will give my dog back to me. Seeing your Riley was almost like an answer to my prayers." He tousled the dog's fur and buried his face in it, too. The joy on his face was almost unbearable to Julian because that is how he would feel if he would lose his dog.

After introductions were made, Julian asked Roy what happened to Riley.

"His death was really caused by old age, I guess. He was going on fifteen, but I just would not accept that it was his time. When he fell down the stairs and seemed not to be in any pain, I knew it was time and three days later we put him down. Hardest thing I ever did in my life. Now, my question is, how did your Riley lose his leg?"

"We were boating in Scotland, and a storm came in, nearly unannounced. The water in the Loch became very wild, and the small boat crashed into an area filled with rocks. A large shard of the boat's hull tore Riley's leg off, and I thought I would lose him, but here he is. I was able to get a prosthetic leg for him a couple of years ago, and that has made his life increasingly more comfortable."

Riley would spend the remainder of the evening bouncing back and forth between Julian, Brian, and Roy, along with begging treats from all the guests.

11

Seeing the empty 'storytelling' chair, a man sat down, and once everyone stopped staring at Riley, he said, "Merry Christmas, everyone. I'm Tom Remely. I'm a teacher and I play guitar and bass for our classic church band at Grace Church here in Bethlehem. I teach computer technology to seventh and eighth graders at Nazareth Middle School.

"I don't remember how old I was, perhaps nine, when 'The Christmas That I Thought Would Be The Best Ever' ended up being the biggest disappointment, and it was all my fault.

"I had decided to stay awake and when the time seemed right go out and peek in the family room. I thought I might catch a glimpse of Santa, but he had already been there and gone, so once again, trying to see him proved fruitless.

I looked around the tree and there, against the wall, was something I had been asking for since I was about seven. My brand-new guitar was setting on a stand, waiting for me to pick up and play. I wanted to do that desperately, but, reluctantly, I returned to my bed, not sleeping the remainder of the night, waiting until everyone was up so I could see my best gift ever.

"When morning came, there was no surprise. Obviously, I still loved the gift, but I wondered if my parents as they eagerly watched for my excitement, saw my regret instead."

"That's what you get for being a stupid kid, Tom." A cookie hit him in the face, and he laughed.

Tom brushed the crumbs from his long-sleeved Dallas Cowboys T-shirt and smiled at his friend. "Do you have a story to tell us, Rich?" He asked as he stood up and found another seat.

12

"Hi, everyone, I'm Rich Ehrhart, and I live in Hellertown. I occasionally sing in the Grace Church classic choir. That's how I know the guy wearing the stupid shirt." He said, "Go Eagles," causing several of the guests to boo, and more to cheer their team.

"I work for Conestoga Construction as a building designer, draftsman. Conestoga is in New Holland, Pa., however, I have the luxury of working from home most of the time. In my free time, I am involved with the youth program at Grace Church Bethlehem, as well as the worship team. I also sing tenor in a community choral group in Emmaus, called the Emmaus Chorale.

"As a child I remember sitting on Santa's lap and asking him for the same two things year after year. Each time when Christmas morning came, I was disappointed to not find either of the two things I had asked for. The two things I kept wishing for were a guitar and a typewriter, thinking this should not be so much of a problem for Santa. Now that I am older and understand what goes on behind the scenes at Christmas, I know that these are not inexpensive things.

"Well somewhere in my teenage years I received both items which was a dream come true, only to find out that I didn't know how to use either one very well. I learned a few chords on the guitar and never took it any further. I knew just enough to get by at a Christmas party one year when I thought it was a good idea to bring the guitar along. Someone asked me to play it and somehow, I faked my way through it, and what I saw was a fun time being had by all those around me.

"I have since given the guitar away to someone else who was looking to learn to play one. Typing, however is a big part of what I do every day now as a draftsman. I am quicker now than I ever imagined I could be. And who knows, perhaps one day a guitar will make a comeback in my life.

"When he stood up, a cookie hit him in the left ear. 'Yeah, and maybe the Eagles will win another Super Bowl in your lifetime.'

Laughter exploded in the room, and the conversation turned to football for about ten minutes.

13

Brian Miller was a little OCD when it came to his house. He saw the cookie crumbs and grabbed the little whisk broom and plastic pan from a painted milk can beside the fireplace. He brushed up the crumbs into the pan and tossed them into the fireplace.

Jeff Wartluft, a member of Roy Clayton's Tuesday morning Bible study group, sat down in the chair after Brian finished. He said, "I'm a retired forester, and I live in Lehighton. My story involves a broom, so this would be a good time to share it, I believe.

"As I was growing up, my father was in sales with Scott Paper Company, and he was transferred many times. The company was always looking to fill empty positions with knowledgeable people. When I was in ninth grade in 1957, that school was my ninth school. Back then my mother, father and I lived in Detroit, Michigan. Christmas was coming. It was our only Christmas there as we lived there just one year. My father was busy in the basement and did not want me down there. He came to me and said that he was trying to wrap a broom for my mother, so she would not know what it was – that's all. It would be a surprise for her. So, I was no longer very interested in what he was doing. And he went to my mother and said that he was trying to wrap a hockey stick for me, so I would not know what it was. He did not want her down the basement either. She became disinterested in this special gift, too. Then on Christmas morning there was this huge wrapped gift next to the tree – weird looking. But I could see that a broom could fit inside. And my mother could imagine a hockey stick fitting in there. My father asked us both to unwrap the gift. That seemed strange, but, oh well. So, you can guess that on Christmas morning, that huge wrapping using paper, and an inner tube encasing a broom and a hockey stick was quite interesting. And it was neat that when my mother and I unwrapped it, there was something for both of us in there. And we were both surprised.

14

Earlier, Wyatt and Grace Nelson took a trip to the Sands Casino, hoping to win a few bucks to help pay for the stuff they were going to need after their son was born. They played for a couple of hours, winning over three grand, and then grabbed a bite to eat.

They took a walk past the Outlets, window shopping, and checking out the Christmas decorations in each store and the huge tree in the center of the mall. Christmas music played from the hidden speakers, and everyone appeared to be in really good moods.

"How are you feeling, honey?" Wyatt asked his bride as he squeezed her hand.

"I feel great, but I am starting to get a little tired walking. Maybe we should head back to the hotel."

"Good idea. So as not to make you walk any distance, I'll go back to the parking deck and get the car and then you can meet me outside."

"Super. I'll watch for you."

When he out of sight, she felt a twinge in her belly, but, because the baby wasn't due for almost two weeks, she just shrugged it off along with the tiredness. When they got back, a nice hot bath and a Hallmark Christmas movie would be a great way to end the night.

She stepped outside, and as she waited for Wyatt, she looked up in the sky. The full moon was shining bright, and it appeared as though a moonbeam was lighting up someplace in the near distance. She thought that pretty cool as Wyatt pulled up and she got in.

15

Randy Mixter, a Vietnam veteran friend of Roy Clayton, was visiting him. Randy lived near Baltimore, and he and Roy also had being authors in common. There was a time when Randy was pouring the books out, and Roy never thought he would catch his friend, but now they were tied. He sat down in the chair and began his story.

"In 1966 Christmas in Vietnam was not the holiday that it was, and still is, in the States. Though the event was celebrated by many in the population, the season wasn't the festive occasion it is here. In Bien Hoa, where, as a military policeman I had town patrol, not a single wreath hung on a door. Not a single Christmas tree graced the shacks that most of the town's residents called home. No decorations of any kind lined the town's main road. Truthfully, Bien Hoa looked the same in December as it did on any other month of the year – seedy and run-down. It was a place where soldiers could find a moment's respite from the war in the many bars that dotted the town's three block main strip.

"Long Binh, the army complex fifteen miles from the town, which served as my home base, wasn't much better. In our company area, there were virtually no signs of the season. A thorough search of the area yielded a solitary Christmas tree in a nearby tent. It was maybe a foot tall and the color of silver aluminum foil, compliments of a caring mother to her soldier son. A few small colored balls hung from its branches along with some spent shell casings and a certainly out of place *Lone Star* beer can. A truly optimistic MP had placed a homemade peace symbol at its peak.

"In the days leading up to Christmas that small silver tree sitting atop a footlocker became a destination of sorts. It wasn't uncommon to find clusters of MPs gathered around it both day and night, often reminiscing on Christmases past and planning Christmases future. In Vietnam the holiday was just a whisper drowned out by the sounds of war.

"On Christmas Eve I was scheduled for Bien Hoa town patrol, an assignment that began at 6 pm and concluded at 6 am the following morning. On this night, as with other nights, Bien Hoa bustled with GIs, either on a short break or leave. As always, a 10 pm curfew was in effect. All soldiers were required to vacate the streets by then. Most went back to their base. Others found refuge in the quarters of some of the more accommodating women of the night. As an MP, I didn't care where they slept. As long as they were out sight, they were out of mind.

As it neared the midnight hour, a fellow MP and I decided to walk the main drag of the now deserted and quiet town. We left the PMO, the Provost Marshall Office, and headed toward the town's outer perimeter. Our trek took us to the end of the small main street where an even smaller road ran perpendicular to it. A right turn at that juncture would eventually lead us to a secure gate behind which stood the massive Bien Hoa Air Force Base. We took a left and were soon wandering through what appeared to be a neighborhood of sorts. Small shacks, most constructed from crushed aluminum cans, crowded the landscape. We were ready to turn back when I heard a sound in the darkness ahead. It sounded like a group of people singing. Intrigued, we marched ahead and soon came upon a church. The contrast between the place of worship and the bleakness surrounding it was stunning. The small wooden structure had an elegance to its appearance, a purity that seemed out of place in this war-torn country.

Here, facing the open door of the church, bathed in the light of its candle-lit interior, the singing had the strength to challenge the night, to silence the sounds of war. We went to the entrance. Inside the townspeople filling the pews listened as a small group of young Vietnamese girls sang a hymn in their native language at the altar. My partner and I watched until they had finished, and in the silence that followed we turned to take our leave. As we walked away, the singing began again.

"Silent night, Holy night...." They began the hymn, singing in English.

I remember turning. Though it was over fifty years ago I remember turning as if it were yesterday. I stood and listened as they sang the entire song, as perfectly as any choir, in any church, in any country. I'm not ashamed to say that a tear came to my eye, and perhaps to my partner's eye also. In those moments as they sang, I was no longer a soldier in a war zone, I was part of a Christmas miracle that I had stumbled across in a torn and tattered town on the other side of the world.

We left not long after that, walking silently, lost in our thoughts. Somewhere in the distance an explosion broke the night's solitude. The Christmas song was louder. I remember thinking that to this day. The Christmas song was louder than the sounds of war.

16

"Hi folks. My name is Michael Larkin. I live in Delaware, but I am visiting family here in Bethlehem. I needed to get some air, so while taking my walk, by the way, there is a full moon tonight and it is gorgeous, I saw the sign by the door and popped in. I didn't think anyone I knew was here, but then I found out that the homeowner is Brian Miller. I worked with him for a period of time at the post office, but I have a veteran story to share.

"I don't remember the exact year but probably 1970 or 71. I was in the Navy and stationed at Newport, Rhode Island. On Christmas Eve, I was hitch-hiking down the Connecticut Turnpike trying to get home to Allentown. It was easy to get a ride in those days especially if you had your uniform on.

"A car pulled off to the side of the road. I ran over to it and saw a couple in the front seat with their two children in the back. Dad asked me where I was going and I told him Allentown, Pa. He said, 'Hop in we're going to Wilkes-Barre.' Chatting back and forth he asked, 'Where in Allentown are you going?'

"I told him, and to my shock they drove me to my front door. I never forgot that family and I think of them every year at Christmas.

"Before I became employed at the Post Office, I worked at Mack Trucks. Many of us were going to be losing

156

our jobs, so several of us decided to take the postal exam to see if we could get a job. I passed and I was hired in July of 1986. A former Mack worker, Frank Bennett, a friend of mine was hired in mid-December.

"He was delivering a route in south Allentown on Christmas Eve, and I had to pick him up because he had no way back to the Post Office. Several years ago, he posted this story on Facebook. I printed it out and I've kept it in my wallet for all these years. If it's okay, I'd like to read it, although it is a bit lengthy.

Since there were no objections, he reached into his wallet, pulled out a folded piece of paper, and began to read.

'My first Christmas Eve as a letter carrier was extremely memorable.

'I woke up that morning to freezing rain, and I knew the weather was going to be like that most, or all, of the day. I was on a paired route, so after I pulled my mail down, I placed it in several canvas sacks. My partner, who had the park and loop route, dropped me off at my first delivery point, and then he went to the green boxes on my route and placed a bag in each one. When I emptied my mail satchel, I would stop at a box and remove the mail from the sack and put it in my satchel.

'As the day wore on, the rain continued to pelt me; and my clothing was soaked through and through. Ice kept building up on my jeans, and I was just totally miserable.

'My partner looked me up when he finished his route and I told him I still had two loops to finish, hoping he would assist me, but it was Christmas Eve and he wanted to get home to his family. He told me that upon his return to the office, he would have someone sent out to either help me or pick me up when I finished.

'Finally, I finished my route and I stood on the corner for a certain amount of time, possibly fifteen minutes or so, until my ride arrived. A patron had allowed me to use her phone to call for a ride.

'I hopped in the Pinto and saw that my driver was Michael Larkin, a friend from Mack Trucks, where we both worked until we knew we were going to lose our jobs, so we both took the postal exam and were hired. He had started a few months before I did.

'He looked at me and said, "Larry, what the heck are we doing this for?"'

'To feed our families, Mike," I replied.

'Mike also said, "You know that because we're PTFs we don't get paid for holidays. Even Bob Cratchett got paid for Christmas."

'When I got home, my family had just left for church. My wife had filled the tub for me, so I took off my wet clothes in the kitchen and literally stood my jeans on the floor.

'I quickly had some hot soup and then jumped in the tub to warm myself a little. Perhaps ten minutes later I hurried back downstairs after dressing for church, grabbled a half a sandwich for the five-minute walk to church. As I left the house, my jeans were still literally standing on the kitchen floor.'

'When we returned home from church almost an hour and a half later, my jeans had wilted, but there was still a three-inch-high ice ring around the bottom of my jeans.'

The story got a great laugh, especially from Brian Miller.

17

On the way back to the hotel Wyatt felt a thump and from the sound thought something may have happened to his front left tire. He pulled over and saw that his tire was deflating. He figured he must have picked up a nail or something sharp enough to puncture the rubber.

He opened the driver's door and said, "Grace, I have a flat tire, so I'm going to have to change it. You sure you're okay?"

"I'm fine. Do you need a hand with this, Wyatt?"

"No. I haven't changed a tire in several years, but I think I can handle it. Just hang loose for a little bit."

He went back to the trunk, pressed the key fob, and opened it up. He shook his head. The trunk was a mess. He had a bunch of old flags he was going to drop off at the American Legion and had forgotten all about them. His dirty golf clubs and shoes were still in there from the last time he played in October. Other junk littered the trunk. He laughed. 'You're a poet and don't know it,' he said to himself. Looking around he couldn't find the jack, then remembering that he loaned it to his brother a couple of weeks ago and never got it back.

"Grace, I can't fix the flat. Can you call for an Uber to pick us up?"

"No problem."

Wyatt sat back in the driver's seat and listened to his wife.

"We can't get one for at least forty-five minutes. Do you want to wait here that long?"

"No. How about a cab?"

Five minutes later she said, "No cabs available, either. Look, its only about six blocks to the hotel. I think I can walk that far, and the fresh air may do me some good. I think I had a little too much to eat."

"Okay, let's do it."

18

Seeing nobody appearing ready to share his or her Christmas story, Brian Miller got everyone's attention, saying, "I had no idea how many guests of either gender would attend our first open house, but Santa left presents under the tree. The tags read Man or Woman, so help yourself to a gift and hopefully the old man figured out what you might want or need."

"Brian, can I have a minute or two, please?"

"Certainly, Russ."

Russ ambled to the storytelling chair and sat down. He pulled out his phone and said, "Yesterday I received an email from a Vietnam vet who wanted to share his story with me. I've been compiling stories from veterans of all eras in anticipation of publishing them in a future book.

"His name is Mark Casey and he worked in law enforcement all of his adult life, concluding his career with the Mission Police Department. Here is his story.

'At Christmas in 1969, my aunt and my mom sent me two big care packages for Christmas. Care packages were always welcome because they usually were filled with items we could not get easily or often. One package was a case of pre-mixed canned screwdrivers and in the other was a gallon bottle of Imperial vodka. Both of these items were strictly prohibited via mail, but somehow, they made it through the inspection process.

'Needless to say, I was the most popular enlisted MP in Lai Khe, a small town about forty miles northwest of Saigon. It was a base camp for the First Infantry Division, and I was in the First MP Company there. We had a great CO and first sergeant, but they did inform me to let my family know not to send anything like that again. We had one hell of a party, and to be honest this is about all I remember about that.'

After Russ stood up, Jessie Miller handed him a wrapped gift, the tag reading, 'To Russ, with all my love.' Inside was a frame with a black and white picture in it, but he couldn't understand what it was for a couple of seconds. When he did, he hugged his wife and gave her a huge kiss. "Folks, this is the greatest gift I have ever received. I'm going to be a father!"

The room erupted in cheers and laughter as they all looked at the ultrasound, seeing Russ and Joanne's baby. Mother and father were absolutely certain they were going to have a boy.

19

Wyatt and Grace were actually enjoying the short walk back to the hotel. The full moon gave off a lot of light, and she still saw that moonbeam shining on something nearby. The Bethlehem Star shone brightly on the mountain. Wyatt seemed not to notice it, not having made any comments.

Electric candles were present in almost every window of the homes where the lights were on. They could see Christmas trees standing sentinel in some of those windows. Most of the homes were tastefully decorated with strings of white lights.

Grace saw where the moonbeam was shining. It was in the front yard of a house only steps away. "Honey, isn't that moonbeam really cool looking?"

Not seeing anything but not wanting to cause a fuss, he replied, "It sure is."

Just at that moment they were standing in front of the house, with a beautiful Nativity scene being washed by the light of a moonbeam. Grace cried out, "Wyatt, my water just broke." She worked her way to the small yard and sat down in front of the manger.

"Help, help!" Wyatt screamed. Men and women hurried from the house to see what was going on. "Is anyone a doctor? Could someone please call 911? My wife is having our baby, but she isn't due until January 7th."

Doc Kethledge and Julian Ross knelt by Grace, who had now laid down on the grass. She was in obvious pain, but both men had delivered babies before, so they guided her through her childbirth.

When she crowned, Doc whispered to Julian, "I don't think this baby is going to make it out by itself. Can you help her get it out?"

He nodded and encouraged Grace when to push.

As soon as the baby was out, Julian said, "Brian, I'm going to have to give the baby the gift or he won't make it," he said in a very low voice.

"Will the child grow up, or be an immortal newborn?"

"I don't know, but if I don't do anything, he will die."

Brian saw Wyatt and called him over. "Can you both hear me?" He whispered.

Grace and Wyatt nodded.

"This man, Julian Ross, is an immortal and he can save your son's life, but we don't know if the child will stay this age or grow up to be a man. If he doesn't help, your boy will not make it to the hospital." The sound of sirens was getting louder every second. "We need to know right now."

Without hesitation the parents to be nodded and whispered, "Yes, save our son's life."

Julian had his knife out and slit the palm of his hand, forcing his life-giving blood into the boy's mouth. Just before the ambulance arrived and the baby was being held by his mother, she felt his warmth, and then he cried.

"Thank you, Julian. We'll let you know what the verdict will be, but I already know. Christian will grow up to be a great man and will help people throughout all eternity." She squeezed Julian's hand, and then the paramedics took over.

Everyone was outside, wondering what exactly happened, and Julian vowed he would tell them all when they went back inside.

Tom Remely strapped his guitar to his chest as he and Rich Ehrhart began to sing *Silent Night.*

About The Author

Larry Deibert is a Vietnam veteran, and he is the first president of the Lehigh Northampton Vietnam Veterans' Memorial, located in Macungie, Pa.

He is a retired postal worker, having hung up his satchel on Leap Day, 2008. After retiring, he worked part time at Lehigh Valley Health Network until retiring in 2016.

Larry is the author of twelve books;
> Combat Boots dainty feet-Finding Love In Vietnam
> The Christmas City Vampire
> Werewolves In The Christmas City
> The Christmas City Angel
> A Christmas City Christmas
> Family
> Fathoms
> From Darkness To Light
> Witches, Werewolves And Walter
> The Life Of Riley
> The Other Side Of The Ridge
> Santa's Day Jobs

He is currently hard at work on his first murder mystery, No Contest, along with several other projects.

Larry and his wife, Peggy, love to travel, especially to beach areas. Last year, they visited Hawaii for the first time.

In his spare time, Larry loves to read, work out at the gym and play golf.

A General's Christmas Carol

1

The men were exhausted. After three weeks of patrolling, enduring nearly unbearable heat, insect bites, snipers, and booby traps, they were ready to celebrate Christmas with three days of rest. In about two hours, they would be at the landing zone, where choppers would pick them up and return them to Firebase Terry. The men could then enjoy hot food, hot showers, and the comforts afforded the men who lived inside the wire for most of their tours.

Lieutenant Edgar Stone, with six months of combat experience, halted his men for a ten-minute break. As he consulted his map, he called up his three best men: men who had been in Vietnam longer than anyone else in the platoon.

SP4 Johnny Johnson, who carried the M-79 grenade launcher, known as the Blooper, had less than sixty days to go on his tour. At nineteen, he was the 'oldest' of Stone's men. He had seen enough combat to last him a lifetime. He sat down on the ground next to Stone and wiped his brow.

SSG Hector Nieves, a career soldier, with ten years in, at the age of twenty-nine, was the platoon sergeant. He sat down on his helmet on the other side of his lieutenant. Hector would be going home in seventy-two days.

A minute or so later, SP4 Myron Rendish arrived. The twenty-year old machine gunner and platoon prankster seemed to always have a smile etched on his face, even during the stress of a firefight. Myron would be returning to 'The World' in eighty-eight days.

Lieutenant Stone said, "Men, the choppers will pick us up in a couple of hours. The map shows the LZ about two kliks away, but the only way to get there in time is to cross the stream. My instincts tell me to take the long way around…"

Rendish interrupted. "Sir, if we take the long way around, there's a good chance we'll miss our ride and might have to hump all the way back to Terry. The platoon is beat up pretty bad."

Johnson agreed with him. "LT, I am plumb wore out and I need to get back to Terry ASAP. I think we should cross. Shit, we haven't seen any signs of gooks in the past five days. I think we'll be okay."

Nieves nodded his head in agreement. "JJ and Myron are right, sir. The rest of the way should be a cakewalk and we all want to be inside the wire on Christmas."

Stone still had doubts. He trusted his men and weighed their opinions before making a decision. He looked back to his weary, under strength platoon, then back toward the stream and the jungle. The LT even looked up as though seeking advice from God, but ultimately, it was his decision to make. He was tired as well and wanted to get back to the firebase as soon as possible.

"Okay, men. We'll take the shortcut through the stream and jungle, but don't let your guard down. Charlie could be out there somewhere, just waiting for us to screw up."

Stone hoped he wasn't making a mistake. Seven of his men had already been evacuated due to the elements and the enemy, fortunately with no deaths. He didn't want to lose any more. It was nearly impossible to get replacements, but he would push hard to get more men as soon as they reached Terry.

2

The twenty-two men of 1st Platoon, C Company, 29th Infantry Division got to their feet. A few minutes later, they waded into the leech-infested stream twenty-five miles northwest of Saigon. Many of the men smiled with relief as the waist high water helped to cool their overheated bodies.

Suddenly, a heavy volume of fire pinned them down in the stream. Thinking quickly, Stone directed his men toward the edge of the jungle. Rendish sprayed the area with hundreds of bullets from his M-60. JJ popped 40-millimeter rounds into the trees, sending thousands of pieces of shrapnel into trunks and branches. Many pieces cut through the leaves and the humid air and into the bodies of enemy soldiers. He was rewarded with screams of pain and the sight of dying NVA.

They fought for their lives for about five minutes, an eternity in combat, until they were finally able to form a defensive position at the edge of the jungle. Three of Stone's men lay dead in the murky water. With the stream at their rear and the jungle to their front and flanks, the twenty-three-year-old lieutenant orchestrated the firefight, directing his men. He barked out orders.

"Vinnie, Tom and Rick! Take the left flank and get behind them!"

Stone looked to his right and yelled, "Jack, Orville and Larry, get around them on the right and put a hurting on the bastards!"

After he issued those orders, he called his radioman over.

"Plantation One, this is Plantation Six. Over."

After three attempts, headquarters responded. "Plantation Six, this is One. Go."

"One, Six. Be advised we are in heavy contact and need gunships. Number of NVA unknown. I have dead and wounded." He gave the map coordinates and said, "Hurry, One. I don't know how long we can hold on!"

"Roger that, Six. Cobras and slicks airborne. They should be over you in forty minutes." The radio operator then added, "Hang in there, LT."

"10-4, One. We'll be home soon. Have beer ready." A wry smile crossed his face as he wondered if they would indeed get home.

Stone watched his men as they made their way into the jungle. When a bullet grazed his cheek, he flattened out in the mud and fired two clips into the vegetation. Stone smiled when he heard a scream.

They battled the NVA for nearly forty-five minutes, desperately low on ammo. Stone then heard the humming of multiple rotors. The choppers plastered the jungle with miniguns and rockets until the enemy broke contact and disappeared into the depths of the jungle.

At the end of the firefight, Stone's command was reduced to fourteen men. Seven survivors were airlifted back to a field hospital. Eight of his men had died on the jungle floor or in the stream. After the wounded and the dead were gone, Stone and the remainder of his men re-crossed the stream to the waiting choppers.

3

Stone loathed Christmas because three of his men died that day. The doctors thought they would survive, but their conditions deteriorated. They died in a field hospital in Vietnam and the only 'family' with them was Edgar Stone, the man they fondly called LT. He prayed to God for hours to save them, but his prayers went unanswered.

4

The general walked the brick pavement. He knew the memorial was huge, but its magnitude did not hit him until he was actually there. Small lights lit the black granite, mirroring his reflection as he passed by. Between the bricks and the granite were gifts left by previous visitors; cans of beer, packs of cigarettes, pictures and letters, small American flags.

No one was in sight at this time of day, and the absolute quiet was perfect for him to reflect upon his past.

When he arrived at the panel bearing his men, he knelt down on the bricks and touched the names of the eight KIAs from that day, asking their forgiveness for not getting them out of the battle alive. He placed one set of his two stars at the base of the panel, rose to his feet, and after assuming the position of attention, saluted those fallen heroes. It was hard to remember their faces after all these years, but memories were beginning to flood his mind. Stone could now see them in his mind's eye-young and full of life-but now they were names on a black wall.

He moved to the next panel and looked at the names of the men who died on Christmas Day.

Specialist Fourth Class Johnny Johnson, from Gainesville, Georgia, was the first name he saw. A smile came to his face as he remembered his 'blooper' man. JJ, as he was called, was the absolute best with his M-79, popping the 40-millimeter rounds and dropping them anywhere the men wanted them. His uncanny accuracy saved Stone's bacon twice. JJ fired the heavy rounds into NVA and VC in close combat.

Before he died, he said to Stone, "LT, I'm sorry I let you down in that last ambush, but I plumb ran out of rounds as that gook came at me with a bayonet."

Stone wiped tears from his eyes and replied, "JJ, you were so brave, and I will never forget you. Ever!"

As those words left Stone's lips, JJ closed his eyes and drifted into eternal sleep, as the LT wept for the man he loved like a brother.

Out of all the letters he had to write for that battle, the one to Vivian Johnson was the most difficult.

He reached up and touched JJ's name, his fingers lightly resting on the engraved letters. After a moment, he pulled his hand away, came to attention and saluted his 'brother'. He then placed a dummy M-79 round at the base of the panel.

170

The next name was Staff Sergeant Hector Nieves, from Altoona, Pennsylvania. Hector left a wife and two sons to carry on without him.

As platoon sergeant, he was a stickler for detail. When his men set in for the night, he checked every defensive position, making sure the men had all their gear in order and their weapons cleaned. Hector had chosen the army as a career to impart all of his military wisdom and savvy to new guys in Vietnam, to give them all a better chance to survive.

He was a devout Catholic and as he prepared to die, he gave Stone the Bible he carried with him at all times. Stone placed the bloodstained Bible at the base of the panel and saluted the brave man's name.

Last was SP4 Myron Rendish, from Grand Rapids, Michigan. His parents and three brothers survived Rendish.

He was the M-60 gunner and he carried the heavy weapon much like the other men would carry the light M-16 rifle. He was 6'3" tall and 225 pounds, all muscle. He was also the platoon prankster who pulled one every chance he could, to keep everyone loose.

The general smiled, remembering one prank pulled on him when they were in the firebase to rest. While Stone slept, Myron squirted shaving cream into his lieutenant's open hand. Then he ticked his face, chest and stomach with a feather. In his sleep, Stone reached up with his hand to brush away the annoying tickle. When he awakened, he found himself covered with white foam, while several of his men laughed like hyenas. He dressed Myron down and had him drop for twenty pushups. After his men left the hootch, Stone giggled so hard he could hardly breathe.

He touched Myron's name and placed a can of shaving cream beside the other 'gifts'. Major General Stone saluted his machine gunner, and then took two steps backward.

Stone knelt down and reached into a pocket of his field jacket. He pulled out a nine-millimeter pistol and placed the end of the barrel to his right temple. A moment before he was going to pull the trigger, he saw his men as they were in 'Nam.

JJ, Hector and Myron stood in front of him, much like Scrooge's specters. Stone blinked his eyes, but his ghosts of Christmas past were still there. JJ walked toward him and said, "Don't do it, LT! You are going to receive a wonderful gift very soon."

He heard Hector and Myron saying, "No! No!"

5

Their voices were replaced by a feminine voice, screaming, "No! No! Don't do it!"

A soft hand rested on his shoulder as he took the pistol away from his temple.

Stone stood up and looked into the eyes of a beautiful middle-aged woman. She was holding a gift to leave at this hallowed place. As he stared at it, he saw that inside the frame were two small pictures and a letter. He looked back at the woman and asked, "May I please see what you are leaving here today? My eyes are not as sharp as they once were, and I forgot my glasses. I need to see the pictures up close. Something about the two men looks familiar."

Hesitantly, she handed her gift to the general, who held it closer to his eyes. Stone saw JJ and his wife posing after their wedding. The other shot was of him and JJ before they went out on that last patrol. He read the letter:

My dearest JJ,

Today I am visiting the memorial for the first time. Several nights ago, I awakened with the feeling that someone was standing in our bedroom. In the moonlight, I saw the shadow of a man. Startled, I turned on the light, but saw no one. I scanned the room and saw our wedding picture lying on the floor, along with the picture of you and the other soldier. I believed it was you who had been standing there.

I knew you were telling me something, and I had the feeling I had to be here today, the day you died. When I looked at the clock on the nightstand, I saw it was 3:30 AM.

I put the photos and the letter inside a frame and brought it here, but I still don't know why.
I love you,
Vivian.

6

General Stone looked at JJ's wife and with a voice fraught with emotion, said, "Mrs. Johnson, I am Major General Edgar Stone, the other soldier in that photograph. I was your husband's platoon commander in Vietnam, and I am the one responsible for his death. I am so very sorry." His head slumped to his chest and he wept.

When he regained his composure, Vivian opened her arms to him. They hugged and she said, "There is no need to be sorry, General. His death was not your fault. JJ wrote often and told me you were the best leader a platoon could have."

They cried in each other's arms for a long time. Afterwards, Vivian placed her gift at the base of the panel next to Stone's gifts. She touched and kissed her husband's name, and then she started to walk away.

General Stone hurried after her and inquired, "May I buy you a cup of coffee and talk with you awhile? I need to tell you how much I loved JJ and how he saved my life."

She smiled and nodded her head.

As they walked away, they never saw the three men in jungle fatigues hugging one another before they were drawn back into 'The Wall'.

Downtime in my hootch in Vietnam, sometime in 1970. My 'kitchen' is to the left with a double burner hotplate.

Made in the
USA
Middletown, DE